THIRTY Y

WRITTEN BY:

R.L. WOODS

ILLUSTRATIONS BY:

JESSI BROOKSHIRE

Acknowledgements

A special thanks to:

Mr. Homer Lusk, Mentor, Friend & Drinking Buddy.
Charles Stafford for being the best damn sounding board for character development and plot-weaving a friend could ever have.
Clayton "Animal" Hickey and Dillion Lescak for leting me dress them up as cowfolk and use them for the cover.

Last, but not least:
To Drew, Cara and the rest of the crew at Catawba Publishing for their friendly help, patience and professionalism.

xXx

Thirty Years of Hate

Copyright 2007 by R. L. Woods

ISBN: 978-1-59712-196-5

Printed in the USA by the Catawba Publishing Company
5945 Orr Rd., Suite F
Charlotte, NC 28213

This book is dedicated to one hell of a man.

Ray L. Woods

My Hero - My Father

Devil, if you're reading this, you can come out of hiding now, for he went up to Heaven.

<u>Disclaimer</u>

This is a work of fiction.

All of my invented characters were not made to represent any persons- living or dead.

The battle of Pea Ridge/Elkhorn Tavern, the battle of Neches/ Cherokee War and "The Trail of Tears" were actual historic events.

Confederate Brigadier General Albert Pike, Chief Bowles, Colonels John Drew and Stand Watie (later promoted to Brigadier General, the only Native American on either side to earn such a high rank, and the last Confederate General to surrender.) were actual historical personages.

Any occurrences, conversations or liberties that I've taken with these events or people, to bring you the best novel that I could possibly write, was done so with no disrespect intended- much to the contrary, I have meant to honor them.

R. L. Woods
Charlotte, NC

CHAPTERS

CHAPTER I

TRICKERY & GUNPLAY

The five outlaws forced the Concord stage to an abrupt halt as it came around the sharp cutback in the hard-packed road.

Tom, the shotgun-messenger, saw them first. Ex-jayhawkers or bushwhackers by the look of them. Men that had used the war as an excuse to kill. Two rifles, a scattergun, and a jumpity kid with a pair of brass-framed Spiller and Burr Navys. They all sported kerchiefs so they wouldn't be recognized. All but their leader.

Tom's attention was fixed on him like a broke-legged hare towards a hungry snake. Although the leader's hands were empty and his manner casual, there was something about him that troubled Tom. Their eyes locked for a slim moment and Tom's fell away as he let the double barreled ten-gauge clatter to the ground.

xXx

Mort looked down from his vantage atop a huge flat-topped boulder that sat cresting the ridgeline of a small spur. The road dog-legged about, between the dry creek bed and the rocky uphill slope.

Caught unawares and outgunned, the stagecoachmen tossed their pistols. With Mort's partners moving in, he was as likely to backshoot one of them as not. It was now their job to finish.

The tension between his shoulder blades eased as he took his finger off the trigger. His disposition was as foul as the brooding storm that had been gathering throughout the day.

The cold of Mort's stony perch had gnawed through his threadbare flannel lohnjohns. He could see the smarts in having a lookout watch over a drygulching, but that didn't change the fact that he was colder than a gravedigger's ass. Gingerly, he propped himself up on his elbows, mindful to leave the Sharps breachloader sighted on the scene below, in case he needed to kill someone in a hurry.

xXx

The passengers and crew started to dismount.

A cowhand with a mustache that drooped past his chin was first out. He took time enough to eyeball the five bandits, to carve each particular into his memory. His Colt was more for varmints than for two legged vermin. He was salty enough to stand up to this lot, but knew full well that his trigger-handling was only good enough to leave him saddled to a cloud and plucking a harp.

At one of the outlaw's prod, the cowhand chucked his pistol into a prickly thicket downslope. He was a mule-headed cuss that didn't take to being told what to do, especially at the disagreeable end of a barrel. Besides, he reckoned, better to have a chance at owning a scratched up gun, rather than a holster-full of air.

Mr. Franks was next. He was tall and willowy. From the beechnut colored longcoat to the polished cedarwood and silver-tipped walking stick, he was as out of place as a fifth ace in a game of high stakes draw poker. A better dressed killer would have been near impossible to find. Or a more soulless one. Stories abound of his exploits that would curl a maggot's stomach.

The professional gunslick stepped out, slow and precise, taking the time to set his matching derby at a jack-deuce angle over his left eye.

Three horse soldiers followed. They wouldn't be issued carbines until they arrived at their duty post. Only the Corporal packed iron in a standard issue flap holster, which he dropped into a limp pile.

Only two women remained within. Neither moved.

"I'll start pluggin' the stage if'n you ladies don't get out double-quick," the outlaw leader ordered as he leisurely drew his own pistol.

A distant echo of thunder rolled in from the North.

The two women emerged. They were as different as a Montana blizzard and an Arizona hot spell.

Señora Isabella de Anza slipped out first. She wore an elegant emerald and pearl dress that highlighted her aristocratic features. She could trace her lineage to a time before her ancestors helped drive the Moors from her homeland. That wouldn't matter once she returned to the city of Calvary, Texas. Nothing would have changed. The stigma of being a onetime working girl and the current owner of the Four Bits, a sinful establishment of refined entertainment, stuck to her tighter than the fine layer of trail dust that covered everything.

The other was Mrs. Hertzig. A shy, unassuming, God-fearing Baptist of Nordic heritage. She wore the simplest of dresses, both in color and cut, that she'd stitched from scratch and mended when called for. Her parents were Georgia Planters who had been able to survive Mr. Lincoln's War and retain most of their wealth, if not their estate. Thirty years earlier, she had married against her mother's objections. Her husband had sent her back to her family at the outbreak of the late unpleasantness. Now, against his wishes, she was coming home because one of her sons, Wesley, was getting married.

xXx

Mort spat out a mouthful of tobacco juice. He watched as the outlaws formed a semi-circle around the passengers.

A quick brutal slap struck his forehead. His hat's sweat-soaked brim smashed into his eyes. The attacker's talon-like fingers used Mort's eyesockets for leverage, yanked the skull upwards and exposed the taut flesh, windpipe and arteries. The razor honed Arkansas Toothpick sliced clean.

Mort was dead before he could wonder why.

xXx

The raid went on, unawares that death had arrived.

"Will ya knobhead'd sidewinders rob us already? 'Cuz, Hell or high water, this stage'll be in Calvary 'fore a single owl hoot," the reinsman drawled.

The outlaw leader laughed. "Didn't come here to *rob* you." He paused. "We're here to kill you."

A couple of passengers recoiled. But not from his words. Their eyes tracked above and behind him.

An instant later it thumped, rolled and sputtered smoke as it struck the ground between the two groups. Fire devoured the fuse that was tightly wrapped around the bundled dynamite. Most stared in disbelief. Chaos reigned.

That's when he struck. Sudden, without warning and from behind. Before the outlaws could react, he stood between two of them. Like the jumpity kid, he held two pistols, but that's where the similarities cut. Arms fully extended outwards until each barrel jabbed against a masked outlaw's head. As the two barrels found outlaw, the two hammers fell as one. Both were dead except for the twitching.

One of the remaining outlaws turned, his rifle swivelled with him. Too slow to save his life. Calmly, the gray-clad intruder put one, then another, bullet into him. His body spun wild, in an attempt to escape the pain. He crushed a bushy thicket as he hit the ground. The outlaw could still breathe, but it was already too late. Like a fish laid out on a riverbank, too weak to survive. Too scared or stupid to just belly-up and drink deep from the perils of eternal damnation.

The unkempt potbellied outlaw couldn't tear his eyes away from the surefire promise of death that the explosives held until a .41 caliber lead ball staggered him back. The shock made his trigger finger bolt down, sending the scattergun's twin loads into the air. It took three more bullets before the pig-like outlaw slumped to his knees, wavered and flopped face first onto the old Indian trail.

The bandit leader cringed with the report of each gunshot, expecting it to be the dynamite exploding, taking his life and leaving not enough of him behind to fill a thimble.

With the lull, he squeaked open his eyes and loosened his breath. Dust from the hard packed earth billowed up into his face. The normally remorseless eyes blazed as the flame disappeared into the heart of the bundle.

CHAPTER II

A GUNSLICK & THE PISTOL FROM HELL

The passengers slowly recovered their wits and tried to understand what had happened. And it wasn't quite done yet.

That's when they saw him.

He stood, like a bronze statue, above the only outlaw still alive. An odd looking, double barreled, over-and-under, Lemat revolver aimed at the crumbled up badman. The hand-cannon's brother was now holstered.

Most of the statue's rig was Confederate issue. His faded butternut trousers had a canary-yellow stripe ran the length of the outside seam. Both knees sported leather patches that were tacked on with little skill. On his aged Tuscaloosa-gray shell jacket were three egg-yoke colored chevrons on each sleeve. A distinction earned through grit and steel.

It was what he didn't wear that was unusual. No hat. No handkerchief folded and wrapped about his head. Nothing slowed the wind from nipping and plucking at his long midnight-black hair. He wore no leather on his feet. Not even the makeshift foot wraps that Johnny Reb had fashioned after his Jeffersons had given up "The Cause."

What struck the passengers was his heritage. He was an Indian, or mostly so. His mother's proud-Cherokee blood forever marked him a "half-breed." It was "his kind" that polite society used in bedtime stories to scare its children into being obedient.

The outlaw leader stood up. Slow, as if he had just awoken from losing a knuckleduster with a fifth of snakepiss. His every motion was matched by the stranger's gun as he looked about at the bodies of his gang. The outlaw was no stranger to war, yet he was still amazed at the flood of carnage that this one man had uncorked as easy as other men drink cheap whiskey and lie.

"Gawdamn but that was slick," the outlaw gave up on flattery, for his words were as worthless as dressing a pig in a twelve dollar petticoat.

A glance up at Mort's perch explained why the redskin was still breathing. A trickle of blood ran down from the rock face where Mort should have been. A ghastly pallor poured over the outlaw's face. The predator had become the prey. His mind slithered about, looking for an angle. He'd never heard of a half-breed lawman or hired killer that packed two such artillery pieces. His mind went back to the uniform.

"Pardner. It's eighteen hundred 'n sixty-eight. War's been done now for nigh on three years."

"This is not about the war."

A puzzled expression crossed the outlaw's face. He shrugged it off with a slight smile that plucked at the corner of his mouth.

"Alright. Take me in," the outlaw said as he put his wrists together and stuck them forward.

"Didn't come here to *arrest* you."

The realization came as the Lemat thundered. The outlaw dug at his guts in a futile attempt to rein in the damage.

He never saw the headshot that followed.

xXx

The passengers started to react. Mrs. Hertzig retreated to the security of the stage. One of the soldiers scooped up Tom's shotgun and scanned the surroundings. The rest slowly approached the carnage and the man who had caused it.

"I'm right beholden to you, Mister," the cowhand said with pure conviction. He stepped forward and shot out his hand as he beamed a toothy smile.

The cowhand's appreciation for life showed in the exaggerated handshake that would've sent a lesser man to the dentist. With the tension broke, Tom and most of the others swarmed in to show their gratitude.

Mr. Franks resettled his derby to the rear of his head. He knew his business. After the initial two shots, the gun's cadence was steady as a drumbeat. A rolling barrage. Accurate. Deliberate. That of a soldier. Yet no match for a professional gun. Franks looked like a rat that had just found a nest-full of unguarded eggs.

"Sloppy handling of lead if you ask me." Franks called out for everyone to hear. "And no hired gun still uses a cap and ball. Too slow to reload."

Franks examined the stranger, to gauge what effect his words were having.

The passengers cleared a space between the two, unsure where this was headed.

The stranger withdrew to a deadly place, without moving.

Mr. Franks continued to goad the man. "And that big horse pistol–" but before he could continue, the grateful cowhand horned in.

"It appears to me that this here man just saved all of our skins."

"It appears to me that the last one," Franks swept off his derby and thrust it towards the leader's corpse, "he murdered."

An unsettled murmur rippled through the listeners. All eyes turned to the stranger.

The half-breed turned on his heel and started to walk away.

"Sergeant, arrest that man!" Mr. Franks demanded of the Corporal.

Osburn thought about correcting the mistake, but the less he was involved with this killer, the better.

The stranger stopped and sat down on his heels at the dead leader's body. He stood up and turned to face the gathering. A gore-covered two shot Remington Double Repeating Derringer held before him. It was small enough to hide almost anywhere, yet it could kill a person just as dead as a heftier pistol, leastways if it hit someplace vital.

Mr. Franks stood his ground as the stranger marched towards him, the Derringer leading the way. The muzzle came to a stop less than a finger's breath from his upturned nose. The stench of blood and bile transformed Mr. Franks. His face drew up ugly and mean. "Sergeant, obviously this man is a Confederate. A renegade. As such, it is your duty to arrest him."

"Madra Dios," the Señora said, her hands flailing wildly for emphasis. "Can't you see that we owe him our lives?"

"If I had wanted your opinion, I would've paid for it," Franks said for all to hear.

Corporal Osburn took off his uniform belt for the second time and tossed it a couple of feet away. "I have no orders and I'm unarmed. Guess you'll have to take care of him yourself."

He was right, in a way. Since the Confederacy packed its bags and gone to the bone orchard, Texas had been under Martial Law. But there was no officer present to bark commands and this dandified butcher was trying to get him killed. A man that couldn't even tell the difference in a soldier's rank.

Mr. Franks yanked his derby frontward and hissed, "This isn't done by far. And you'd best not use one of those stingy pistols on me," his eyes flickering to the derringer and back, "because I'll make you eat it."

The little pistol answered with an audible click as the half-breed thumbed the hammer back and hooked the small front bladesight inside Mr. Franks' nostril. Without breaking eye contact, the stranger used his free hand to acquire the all but forgotten walking stick.

Mr. Franks' ugly and mean melted away like a snowball in Hell and all that was left was a need for destruction.

The cane's silver tip tapped about the longcoat three times. Outside hip. Outside hip. Under the left arm. The stranger threw away the cane, reached inside the coat, and pulled out a pistol.

He could see that this was no cowboy's lead-spitter, but a Remington New Model Army revolver, custom altered to accommodate metal cartridges. The trigger assembly had been removed and the hammer spur was slicker than pig lard on a red hot skillet. Nothing slowed the pistol's hammerfall once it was let go by thumb slipping or fanning with the outside palm edge of the other hand.

Tom let out a long, low whistle.

The half-breed's inspection continued as he carefully rotated the pistol.

The barrel was special-made to right under five inches; harmful to accuracy, but sweet on gun speed. The front sight was removed so as not to hitch up as the six-shooter was readied. A "U" shaped slice was carved out of the lower right side of the recoil shield to load single bullets without pulling the cylinder and the loading lever was converted into a shortened ejector rod.

The name engraved on the barrel said it all; Nemesis. The Indian backed off a few paces, turned, and walked away, pistol and all.

Mr. Franks' eyes scurried about until he saw what he was looking for, rushed to the outlaw leader's corpse and grabbed for the unused Colt.

Metal snapped on metal from behind Mr. Franks. He froze at the first sound as if Medusa herself had played peaky-boo with him.

"I wouldn't do that if I was you. Around here folks don't shoot people in the back."

Franks would've recognized that stupid cowboy's voice anywhere after sharing the stage with him for the longest three days of his life. "So you can't shoot either."

"Don't you remember me telling you?" the cowboy said with pride, "I'm from Tennessee."

Franks hadn't quite made up his mind until he heard the shotgun's second hammer made ready. The Colt was left alone.

The driver reclaimed his seat and arranged the leather straps between his stubby fingers. Once settled, he told Mr. Franks and the Cowboy. "Might as well curry-comb a frog as ta 'spect any sense from you-all. Both you-uns better git as quiet as a tick, or you'll both be wearin' out your boots and wavin' at our backsides."

"We can't just leave the bodies," Isabella said, hoping to restore some decency. It was directed towards the Corporal, the apparent legal authority, who was diligently looting the dead.

No one else took to answer her. Most of the passengers were too busy, looking for gold fillings among the dead or scanning every bush and rock for more outlaws.

The cowboy returned from downslope with his pistol. He was blowing out the dust and wiping it down, not too much worse for the whole of it.

The driver sat in a bitter stew as time rolled and the stage didn't. "We're burning daylight down ta a nub and cinder."

Tom looked off in the direction the butternut and gray-clad Indian had taken. "Guess he just up and left us?"

And I say good riddance," Franks said bitterly.

Tom got his shotgun back from the cowboy as he asked Franks, "Why are you so hellfire bent on hating this man?"

"Where do you think the Indian came from?"

"I dunno, I'm just glad he was here."

"Did you see how easy he got the jump on them? Or how they didn't shoot at him?" Franks continued. "Or that he was standing with them when this all started?"

"What are you getting at?"

"You don't think he just stumbled onto these men and decided to attack them? And for what?"

"He is a godsend," Isabella added.

"What would a whore know about God!"

She said nothing, but her rage clearly showed in her face and the trembling of her hands.

Mr. Franks went back to his conversation with Tom. "He's one of them, I'd wager. Probably decided to kill them and rob the bodies once we were gone."

Tom's only reply was to wag his head "no." He couldn't understand what Franks was trying to get at exactly, for three days, the killer hadn't voiced his mind on anything. Not politics. Not religion. Not even the War. And, Tom wondered, if the outlaws knew that Franks was carrying his pistol....

"Thank goodness we have Corporal Osburn here to see to their belongings," Isabella said to no one in particular.

Tom laughed. So did the cowboy. Isabella wasn't winning any friends among the soldiers, but she didn't care. Being a social outcast had its advantages.

Franks was about to continue, but he noticed that he had lost their attention. He looked up and saw their deliverer, atop the cliff face. Motionless. A war god looking down upon a recent battlefield. Franks was uncomfortable under the Indian's gaze. In some ways smaller. And it burned.

The Indian wore shoes now. A hat too, low crowned and wide brimmed. Originally black, but between the sun, dust and sweat, it looked stitched from plowed mud. He disappeared from the edge and the dead outlaw-rifleman was unceremoniously pitched over the ledge. Mort's body sounded like a wet sack of dishes and guts when it struck the ground.

A stunned silence followed. It was a practical way to get a corpse down from such a place, but some regarded it as a hardhearted act.

"God works in mysterious ways," the cowboy offered, a wide grin peered from behind its woolly canopy.

The rail-thin, tight-lipped Private brought in the outlaws' string of horses. Tom and Corporal Osburn started to cinch the dead to their saddles. Slow work, made all the more so with Osburn's rifling through each saddlebag and Tom's not being strong enough to lift an objection.

"Northerner rollin' in. Time's a'wastin'." The driver tried a new tack to hurry them along.

"Holy blessed Mother of Christ!" Tom stumbled back from the remains of the last bandit.

Osburn had removed each outlaw's kerchief as he prospected for dental gold.

The men gathered. They saw what had been a youthful looking boy still lying where he fell, an unfired pistol in each cold hand. Death had taken him in an instant, without bothering to scrape the look of excitement from his face.

"The Reb's good as dead."

The cowhand scratched his head and gave a puzzled look.

"That's Toby. Mrs. Hertzig's youngest." Tom jabbed a thumb back over his shoulder towards the stage.

Mrs. Hertzig erupted from inside the coach. She knocked over one soldier and made another scramble in her charge to reach her son's lifeless body. Tears were flowing before she arrived to hold her baby. There were no hysterics. No screams of denial. No trying to barter with God to change what had happened. No apparent hatred. Just a mother's grief for the loss of her child.

The driver shook his head. "Hertzig will be mad enough to eat the Devil, horns and all. It ain't *if* the Major will kill him, but how many times."

"Reb's good as dead," the cowhand echoed quietly, more to himself than to the others.

CHAPTER III

BRUTUS, A CALICO & A TIN STAR

The stranger rode into the little town of Calvary from the East, through darkened side streets. Nothing greeted him but the shadows that grew in the waning light.

He pulled up at a quiet livery. It had no signboard proclaiming its trade. No oversized wooden cut-out hung from a timber and a couple links of rusted chain. Four walls and a roof over stalls and horseshit made it plain.

He banged on the door while still astride his McClellan saddle. The livery's sun-grayed lumber rattled and shook under the assault as dust leapt out from every which where.

A clamor of movement and muttering came from deep within the A-frame. Wood scraped on wood as the door latch was drawn. The door groaned open and out stepped a jowly, aged black man with more pepper-colored hair on his face than atop his head. His merchant's smile burnt away as he looked up at the rider.

The creeping darkness blended with the man's soiled hat and uniform's gray, outlining a fearful image.

21

He knew this rider. Not even the sight of Moses, holding the Ten Commandments on his doorstep, would have surprised him more. Six years had passed since then. And Father Time had only seen fit to visit the man's clothes.

The big bay tossed his mane, pulling the liveryman's attention from the rider to the mount. The horse had a crop of old scars that spoke of Minié balls and sword cuts. Yet the chestnut's eyes blazed with an intensity that had only grown with all he endured.

The stableman removed his straw hat and worked the brim with both hands. In a voice too small for his girth, "You come here to kill me?"

"I came to board my horse."

A bristle of teeth poked through the former slave's, now livery owner's, chin whiskers. "Yes Sir, I rightly will. Come on in and I'll take right good care of you." He paused, rubbed his chin and grinned. "You ain't gonna pay in graybacks is you?"

"The war is over, Brutus." The rider dug into his pants and answered the question by flipping a gold coin to the old man.

The stableman caught it, paused and paled. Slowly, he turned his gaze downwards. A half eagle. Five dollars. Its weight, like the horseman himself, was almost too much for him. Sometimes gold, like men, have a history that can not be escaped.

"My name's Isaiah now. I chose it after I was freed," he said as he walked up, set the coin reverently in the rider's hand and used both of his to close the other man's fist about it. "Your money is no good here. Come on in. I'd say we have a lot to talk about, but you never were one much for talk."

"Where is the Ambrose?"

"Straight behind you," Isaiah told him, "but *you* can't go in there."

xXx

"No Indians allowed," the clerk behind the counter firmly stated.

The stranger pulled the Ambrose's door shut behind him as he entered.

"No Negroes. No Heathens. It's hung on the signboard right out front."

The intruder ambled forward as if he hadn't understood.

Enos sighed as he leisurely reached under the counter top. Cudgel in hand, he straightened upright, but the club wouldn't move. Part of him was nagging away without letting up, like his wife. Decades of experience whispered their warning, forcing him to take a closer look at this man.

The stranger came to a halt a good yard and a half away from the desk and slid a long wooden box across the counter top. A pair of worn-to-death soldier's lace-ups were shadowed over by a double breasted military greatcoat that was older than the Book of Revelations. Deep-dark leather pommelbags rode his left shoulder. The former reb was too far back to do counter business. He stood easy. Poised. Ready for whatever a silk cravat-wearing, henpecked, citified ink-pusher could pull up from behind a hotel desk.

Enos let go of the club as if it had turned foul in his grip. "I'll get the owner."

True to his word, within a few minutes Enos trailed Sara Mae back into the lobby. Eyes downcast, he humbly resumed his post behind the counter.

Ms. Sara was small and lean. In her late-twenties, she had earned every inch of what was hers with savvy and resolute energy. Her attire matched her physical charm. Functional. No frills. Yet as easy on the eye as a sunset on a fine Spring day.

"Ma'am," the stranger said with a hint of his childhood Georgian drawl as he tipped his hat.

"Enos here says you're giving him a hard time," Sara accused the stranger as she fixed him through her oval shaped spectacles.

"Just trying to get a room."

"He told you that I don't allow Negroes or Indians?"

"Yes, Ma'am."

"Then why are you still here?"

"Just trying to get a room."

Ms. Sara took in his measure. This was no simple tenderfoot dressed in Confederate cast-offs vying for table scraps or begging for loose change. Or a young fool buck that had slipped away from the reservation looking for excitement. He was as real as death.

Good manners changed nothing. Trouble would find him, and those about him.

"I simply can not allow you to stay here."

The Cherokee remained composed and pulled out the same five dollar coin and laid it on the counter.

"I don't want any trouble," Sara said in a practiced response, "but I will send for the Sheriff."

The stranger listened to her talk as he reached into his pommelbags. Both of the townsfolk scarcely had time to get nervous before the stranger pulled out a letter and laid it on the thick hotel register. Without taking his eyes off Sara, he picked up the coin and placed it on the letter.

Sara moved forward. Her hand covered her lips. The envelope showed water damage and fraying, but the writing was unmistakably that of her husband.

"Where did you get that?"

"I will tell you in the morning."

Her resolve softened as her gaze went from the letter to the hard lines of the Indian-rebel-stranger.

"No liquor?"

He said nothing. Just gave her a look that both answered her question and made her feel somehow foolish for asking.

She picked up the letter. "I feel it in my bones that I'm going to regret this. Enos, give him number seven."

"We will continue this discussion after dinner," Sara commanded over her shoulder as she departed back the way she had come.

"No Ma'am, in the morning."

Enos was fit to be barreled in brine, but Sara had given him his marching orders and he went about his duties. The coin slid into the money box and the sign-in register was pushed forward.

"Make your mark." He turned and plucked a key from a row of nails. "Number seven is up the stairs, last door on the left."

The Indian was at the top of the stairs before the clerk looked down. "Hey, what kind of chicken scratch did you put in my ledger?"

"It is written in Tsa-la-gi."

Enos eyed him with suspicion. He had never heard of such a thing. "What's that?"

"The language of my people."

The clerk grew more cynical as he bug-eyed the irregular lettering. What's it say?"

"Heathen."

xXx

The stagecoach's arrival was a somber one. Hours late and six saddle mounts tied single file to the stagecoach's rear boot. Five of them carried men, belly down and wrapped in blankets. A painted mustang, Toby's mount, was the only horse J. D. Taylor recognized. The empty saddle sent a cold spell clean through Calvary's only lawman.

Sheriff Taylor met them at the edge of town, where he had been waiting. Tom saw him first and stopped just shy of hollering out. He noted the grim set about the Sheriff. The steel-framed Henry rifle cradled in the nook of J. D.'s elbow was a stark statement.

The Sheriff escorted them the rest of the way into town. By the time they'd pulled to a stop in front of Cartman's store, Tom's version of the attack had grown so that the facts were only somewhat included.

Taylor seemed unruffled by the account until he found out what he had already suspected. Toby Hertzig was among the dead.

The passengers filed out amid a sea of disorderly townsfolk who had flocked about.

"I'm plumb sorry about the loss of your son. Would you like me to take you out to your family tonight?"

Except for the silent tears that still flowed past her tight-set lips, Mrs. Hertzig was holding up fairly well on the surface. Blood and bits of her son had dried to her dress and one side of her face. She had cradled him the rest of the way in the coach. Only Mr. Franks had objected, but to no one's worry.

"That won't be necessary. I'll be staying the night at the Ambrose."

J.D. was not surprised. "I'll ride out at first light to tell the sorrowful news to the Major." He looked down, awkward for what else to say.

"Thank you for your kindness, Sheriff."

The Sheriff turned to the dapper dressed Easterner. "Franks." It was a statement of fact. Not a question of identity.

The dandy said nothing.

Sheriff Taylor called his play and waited.

"Have we met?"

"Nope. But I've been introduced to your pistol. It's back at my office right now. Right fine shooter," He said with a smug look about him.

"Can I have it back?"

"Well that all depends on you. Let's go over to the jail. You answer a few questions, I'll give it back to you tonight."

"And if I don't?"

"I'll have it sent to you once you reach the next town."

Franks didn't think it over long, "Lead on, Sheriff."

The Sheriff headed away from the growing clamor that always arose when civilized people had an opportunity to gawk at brutality. Franks shook his head and turned his attention back to the lawman.

The killer entered the jail first and was immediately struck by the smell of the place. It wasn't overwhelming, merely all too familiar. The dust and stale coffee of the front office lost out to the reek from human misery and weakness from the cells in the back.

He had seen much worse. Backwater mining camps where the jail was a chain wrapped around a stout tree. Towns too small or too poor for the law, where the towners would catch a wrongdoer and barricade him in an outhouse until they had drunk up enough courage to decide the scoundrel's fate.

J.D. closed the door and hung his John B. on a wall peg.

"Coffee? Made fresh this morning."

Franks shook his head and looked about. The jail had the Sheriff's mark on it. Sparse and orderly. Only the addition of Homer, Virgil and Melville to the standard dog-eared King James, seemed out of place. That, and in a tidy stack, more paperwork than a church has sinners.

"So. He's been here?"

"Nope. Had a local drop it off. Told me that its owner was on the stage. Soon as I saw the shooter, I knew who I was looking for."

"What have you heard?"

"Nothing good. That you're a paid killer. A costly one at that," he said as he put the Henry in a rifle rack. "You cut the law to the bone, but don't break it. Or leastways ain't been caught at it yet." The Sheriff plopped into the buffalo hide chair behind his desk. "That mess up in Montana Territory would've seen you swing. If you'd have left anyone alive to testify."

Franks said nothing. He knew that the Sheriff held the winning hand. No bluff would work.

J. D. leaned forward and opened the desk drawer with his left hand. He placed Nemesis on the desktop.

"I'd feel better about reaching for my pistol if you'd take your fingers off whatever you've got wired up under there."

A vulgar smile crossed the Sheriff's face. He leaned back in the chair and made a show of interlocking his fingers behind his head. "Go ahead. Pick it up."

The gunslick did just that. Pulled out each shell and stood them in a row on the desk. Then he gave Nemesis an all-around inspection that ended with thumbing the hammer back six times to check each hammer notch. The pistol settled into his hand then took off. Transformed into a blur of spins and rolls, bordershifts and pinwheels. It was a display of precision. Magical. A deadly warning.

"You're free to go."

CHAPTER IV

THREE REASONS, FOUR CARDS & ONE TAUNTING

Franks reloaded Nemesis with fresh bullets from deep within the longcoat. It slid smoothly back into the leather-lined pocket. He started to leave, but paused in the doorway.

"Hey Sheriff, you didn't relly ask me anything. Why are you letting me walk out of here so easy?" The Sheriff thought for a moment. He had found out all he needed to know without asking. "Three reasons," he said as he slid the unwanted bullets into the drawer.

"You ain't broke any law yet, so I can't hold you. You and I both know that I can't beat your gun-handling. But I'm the Sheriff, so I reckon that I don't have to. You hurt any of my people and you'll have a twenty man posse so far up your ass that you won't be able to button your shirt."

The gunman shook his head slightly as a trace of a smile appeared. He turned to leave, then stopped. "And the third?"

"Well son, what you did up in Montana Territory was plumb evil, and it may not be Christian-like, but it might be a good thing for you to be pissing on brush fires in Hell."

"What makes you think he's good enough?"

"You got your pistol back."

xXx

Buckley Hertzig stood unseen in the deep shadow cast by Cartman's false storefront as the stagecoach arrived. He waited for the johnny-law to walk away with the Eastern fop before he stalked through the assembled townsfolk.

His mother waited within the fold of the crowd.

"Ma?"

She answered with a resounding slap to her oldest son's face. Mrs. Hertzig was not one for public outbursts. A consideration which made it all the more shocking to those who stood in mute witness. She walked away before anyone was able to say a word, leaving behind a confused and violent little boy sheathed in a man the size of a small mountain range.

Buck retreated, but only as far as the Four Bits. A house of cardinal sin and other unrestrained amusements. It was built on a small rise, more than four hundred yards northwest from the closest building of the town proper, that being the First Baptist Church of Calvary.

At town meetings, every respectable townsman would label it as a Palace of Sodom, a blight upon their fair city, but they would pass no new ordinance against it. And shortly thereafter spend a goodly part of their wages within its splendor.

From a distance, only the bars on the windows made it look any different than any other two story hotel. Bars kept suitors out, would-be "couples" from eloping with the Madam's feminine investment, and those who would rather not pay after partaking of a lady's company were forced to leave by the front doors. And nobody left without paying.

The music coming from inside made Buck all the more disagreeable. It wasn't the professor's romancing of the ivories that badgered him. Or that the pianoman was one of those circus freaks. Blind, and too much the tomfool to act like it. Everything from walking around without stumbling about to flipping his sheet music as he played.

What got Buck's goat was the brand spanking new, lavishly carved, Steinway & Sons cottage upright. It was a replacement for the rosewood Cadby vertical that *Miss* Isabella held Buck accountable for. A former blue-belly had made the mistake of arguing with him about the Siege of Vicksburg. Both were liquored-up and spouting political rhetoric that neither one of them actually understood, but were willing to die for nonetheless.

The Billy Yank drove home his point with General Grant's success.

Buck replied with ivory and steel. Followed by an abolitionist skull being introduced to the London piano's inner workings. The instrument was repaired, but the stench of death lived on.

The fracas was called self-defense. Didn't even rate a circuit judge. But Señora de Anza had not allowed him back in until he, or rather his father, had paid for the damages.

Inside was positively decadent with finery, both in furnishings and the ladies themselves. As fate would have it, there were twelve "boarders" working for Isabella. A few were actually beautiful, most were not. But each one had something special.

Buck hooked his boot on the bar's brass footrail. He grumbled, and drank. Challenged anyone who drew too near. And drank more. The working girls knew the healthiest course was to steer wide. Only the bartender came by, and then just to put another bottle down.

Buck had destroyed a pondful of tonsil varnish before he slowed up a bit. With the bleary picture of clarity that the whiskey had unleashed, Buck chewed over what had happened and what to do about it. He had overheard some of what Tom had told the Sheriff and what the other passengers had said to the crowd. His brother was dead. Now his mother was sore at him. And it was all due to some renegade Indian's doing. He would kill this Indian.

"Hey, Buck, you sumbitch," came a voice from behind, "wanna lose some money?"

Buck twisted about. He wasn't in the mood. But Longhorn, Dogbite and Sal were the only few critters that somewhat resembled friends to him.

Longhorn was a gangly, odd angled, buck-toothed blight of a man. It was his ears that had earned him his nickname. Small children could take shade beneath them. It wasn't just their size, but that they veered out like the horns of his namesake.

Dogbite was a mouthy, pugnacious, dough-faced Scotsman who looked as if he'd broken up more than one straight razor fight with his face. His beard was long and without redemption, something a big city rat wouldn't curl up to die in. He would rather marry a rattler than wrap his tongue around a single word of truth. The piss-poor thing about it was that nothing he said was near believable. Claimed that a dog bit him once and three days later the dog up and died. People had called him "Dogbite" ever since.

Then there was Sal. His name was shortened from an old world one that used most of the alphabet twice and three times on Sunday. Born on the outskirts of Italy's capital, he was never able to shake the look of a goat farmer who had murdered a cowboy for his clothes. The runt of any litter he ever stood with. Quiet, until he saw a chance to say something hurtful. And he never passed up a chance. Sal always shuffled cards like an old man makes love. Slow and not very well. But one couldn't say much, because he dealt even worse. On Sal's turn, each of them had come up with their own routine.

Dogbite would cuss himself dry. Sal would stop until he had finished, then continue as if there had been no interruption.

Longhorn would fold his hands and use them as a pillow for his sloping forehead until all the cards were dealt, pick them up and utter a contemptuous "Sumbitch," regardless of what he held.

As for Buck, he would grab up each card as it came, as if his intensity would scare the deck into being lucky for him.

Ace of Spades. Buck smiled and took another swig of whiskey.

"I heard about Toby," Sal said. "Guess you're all broke up about it, huh?"

Buck didn't look up from his cards, "Deal." He was in a dark humor, and any attempt to get him wishy-washy would only be an annoyance at best.

Sal knew it.

And it brought a smile to his lips.

Ace of Clubs. Buck's well oiled poker face lit-up.

"Heard if we're going to have the wedding or the funeral first?"

"I don't know. Deal the damn cards."

Three of Hearts.

"Aren't you suppose to be taking your momma someplace?"

All at the table knew the Major had ordered Buck to fetch Mrs. Hertzig out to the Circle 9. The son had failed his father. Buck catching a mean case of bottle-fever wasn't going to help a tick.

Longhorn sat upright. Dogbite chuckled through his unlit cheroot.

Two of Diamonds.

Heard your mommy gave you a peck on the cheek."

Buck skipped his last down card and seized the little Roman, his burly hand wrapped from ear to ear, and started to squeeze.

"I noe wer hee iz."

Buck paused a moment, but still couldn't figure out what the little man meant, and resumed crushing.

"He said he knows where the sumbitch that killed your brother is hiding," Longhorn loosely translated.

CHAPTER V

DEATH, HONOR & THE LASH

7ᵗʰ of March, 1862. The Civil War was in its second year. Just North of Leetown, Arkansas, at a place that would come to be know as the Battle of Elkhorn Tavern to Southerners, but to the North it was the Battle of Pea Ridge.

Albert Pike was an immense man with a Zeus-like beard and a zealot's eyes. He looked more the part of a fire and brimstone sermonizer than that of a secesh Brigadier General. An imposing man when calm. Frightening on a day like this.

Pike had been ignored, neglected and delayed by the Richmond brass and bureaucrats until they reluctantly signed alliances between the Confederacy and the Five Civilized Tribes. It took until mid-February before he was able to return to his new command.

With red tape and intolerance behind him, he looked forward to repelling the Republican invaders. But that was not to be. The Fort Smith Quartermaster had not supplied his Indian troops. Most had showed up with a fighting spirit and little else. They needed food, shoes, rifles and everything else a military unit requires. Orders came in, before anything could be done, to move his command into Northwest Arkansas.

A blizzard had hit three days earlier, forcing his woefully equipped and untrained men to trudge across a wintery hell of frigid streams and tangles of felled trees, courtesy of the Federal Army.

On top of it all, he'd promised the Indians that they would only be used to defend their own territory. He was a man of his word, and it galled him that he was forced to break it. A man that was an "oath breaker" could easily wind up all sorts of dead. The Cherokee had a whole set of rules about declaring a feud, but once begun the fixed price was a life. They called it "Blood Law."

Of the tribes, the Cherokee fielded the largest force. Enough to muster two separate units, with two separate commanders. They were divided further as one of the units was made up of full-blooded "pins" who wore gray, but their sympathies ran blue.

A nearby rifle report brought General Pike's thoughts back to the present. He listened as both Cherokee leaders continued their bickering within range of the Union artillery position. This only fed the General's months of pent up frustration.

"We have no orders to advance and we'll be killed," complained John Drew. The two crossed pins on his lapel showed his affiliation, if not his Colonel's rank.

"We don't need to wait for written orders from McCulloch or Van Dorn," Colonel Stand Watie said in a patient tone. "If General Pike says we attack, we attack."

"We are untrained...." Drew's voice trailed off.

Watie scoured him with his eyes. "If you don't want to fight you shouldn't be here."

Another shot rang out from the same location.

"Stop wasting your powder," Pike shouted.

Both Colonels quit their exchange. Drew looked startled at the General. Watie held for Drew's answer.

The General looked down, brows knitted, as he pondered what to say. Pike understood that this rift endangered his entire command. If he was going to achieve anything during this war, he'd have to establish

36

his authority right then and there. An uneasy quiet rose up between them. He cleared his throat to speak when a rifle fired yet again.

General Pike charged down upon a small clump of his soldiers positioned behind a rail fence. Both Watie and Drew glanced at each other and then followed in the General's backwash.

Pike slowed at the odd sight before him. Several mixed bloods and even one of his Texans were busily reloading their Springfields, but apparently only one man was actually firing. Disobedience from an enlisted. How could he get two Colonels to listen to him if he couldn't even get this one Private to do so?

Without turning from his prone position, the soldier handed the empty longarm to the Texan waiting to exchange it with a fresh rifle.

"Low and a mite left," the switchman said.

The Brigadier General looked down at the offending Private. Pike's Indian troops were made up of painted faces, colored turbans and feathers jabbed into floppy wool hats. Clothing ranged from a buckskin loincloth to Eastern tailoring. Even among such an unusual outfit, this man stuck out like an honest politician.

Underneath a dust and sweat covered Stetson was an average-sized man, maybe even slightly smaller, with waist-long black hair. The General could make out little else about him, other than that he became as still as death before taking a shot.

The Private wore the remnants of a brick-red uniform jacket that looked more at home squaring off against Napoleon's La Grande Armee, some fifty years gone, than against Lincoln's Federal Army in the Arkansas countryside.

A wickedly curved saber was strapped crosswise across his back. It wasn't the regulation issue "wrist breaker" that gentlemen and cavalry strapped to their hip, but three feet of Prussian-forged steel. A short rifled flintlock leaned against the rail fence next to him.

"Maybe you can't hear me," Pike yelled. "I gave you an order to stop firing!"

"Maybe you did not hear me," the man said as he aimed once again, "over the incoming cannon-fire."

The General's face darkened with rage. His mouth fell open as he puzzled over the rifleman's words. He stepped back and eyeballed the length of his line. Most were lying low and looking towards the enemy troops. But a few were playing cards or joking about. The General could clearly see more than one soldier using his knapsack for a pillow.

"My 'glass, and be damned quick."

The Private fired once more.

A prim and plumed junior staff officer quickly presented the long brass scope, segments already extended for viewing.

The General took in the Union position, paying careful attention to the field pieces set in the woodline. He could see very little movement around the guns. Nervous little blue capped heads poked out from around a tree or from behind a fallen comrade. There was a soldier all tore up and twisting about a gut wound. No one ventured to aid the slowly dying man. Or manned the guns.

Pike also noticed that a gap had formed between the battery and the cavalry deployed to protect it.

"Can you keep them off those cannons?"

"No."

"No?"

"I can keep firing. They can keep dying."

"That's good enough for me," he said as he pulled out his pocket watch. "Colonel Watie. Colonel Drew. Prepare your men. We charge in two minutes."

xXx

Private Morgan Black continued to fire as men and mounts flattened the rail fence. Lone Star rebel yells mixed with traditional war whoops as they surged forward.

The Union pickets wavered, uncertain, then broke without scarcely firing a shot. The fleeing pickets took the Union cavalry with them. Only the lightly armed artillerymen remained.

A Gun Sergeant made a dash for a firing lanyard, but a rifleshot whined off the gun tube, he turned heel and joined the rout.

The fight around the battery was quick, brutal and one-sided.

The charge ended at the guns. Morgan watched as enemy dead were riddled with bullets. Knives and tomahawks flashed. General Pike was in the middle, screaming for them to stop. He was ignored as they danced about. Several rode a cannon barrel as if they were at some macabre rodeo. They piled straw about the retreating Gun Sergeant's field piece.

Morgan watched. A group of pins caught his eye. All four faces were uniformly painted red. They squatted and listened as one gave orders with excited hand signals. Morgan's eyes tracked out the path of the gestures.

"Are they all loaded?"

"Yup," answered the rifle-exchanger.

"Get ready."

The pins spread out, careful and slow. Coyotes stalking an aging mountain lion.

Their leader's full concentration went into getting into position without being discovered. He was proud of what he was about to do for his people. After the white man's war was only a bitter memory, his name would still echo in the council houses.

He hadn't noticed that he alone still advanced. Or that the other three were already dead.

A bullet slammed into a tree between the pin-leader and the Colonel. Surprise was lost as Stand Watie turned about. The experienced warrior understood the situation faster than the pin could adapt to his plan's failure. Watie's pistol-ball left the assassin clawing war paint and writhing in agony.

xXx

Three days had passed since Cherokee had fired on Cherokee during the first day of battle. The incident had raged between the two factions, not just the fine marksman who stood shackled before the General inside the confines of the General's wall tent.

This was Pike's first good face-to-face with the rifleman. For all his skills, he was wholly unremarkable in build or stature. He wasn't actually ugly, but his looks wouldn't inspire poetic verse either. His face was that of well-tanned stone, smooth, yet set to reveal nothing. The General had seen this facade affixed on career soldiers and countless Indians. A Greek-like stoicism that drew a picket line between the man and the outside world.

Not so with this man. It was natural. Real. Not even a part of him, but more a reflection of his inner strength. Somehow, Pike felt safe in his presence.

The General wondered if the reverse was true. What it must feel like to be this man's enemy? The thought was unsettling to the more than three hundred pound man. He knew what he had to do, but he was going to be damn careful going about it.

The plumed staffer opened the canvas flap. "General," the Lieutenant announced, looking as if Saint Nicholas had just departed, "it's all here."

"Thank you. That'll be all." Pike waited until the officer was well away.

Colonel Watie sat to one side of the General. Brutus, Albert Pike's bodyguard, servant and slave stood next to the prisoner.

The one-star addressed his prisoner. "Three days ago, I was ready to have you whipped for ignoring my orders. Then, I was ready to slap Sergeant's stripes on you." Pike went on, "Now Colonel Drew demands that you stand before a firing squad."

The General paused. He hoped for a reaction to his words. He gave up quickly when he realized that it would make more sense to hold his breath until Christ's second coming.

Brutus took a step forward to speak, but Pike held up his hand to stay any interruption.

"All of this was solved when Colonel Watie reported that you were dead."

"He must have healed up some," Watie stated as pure fact.

"Brutus tells me you saved him from a handful of deserters."

"Only two," Morgan said.

Only two, Pike thought. He made it sound so easy. Unleashing death seemed to come natural to him. The General looked down at the table covered in maps, letters and his polished silver flask. "The army payroll Brutus carried was over sixty thousand dollars in gold coin."

General Pike rapidly scribbled and signed a letter. "Brutus, you will leave this camp a free man." He slid the letter aside.

Pike turned his attention back to the prisoner and started in on a virgin sheet. "If you stay here, the pins will surely kill you, so I'm going to transfer you to a North Carolinian unit where I know the commander personally."

The General used his fingers to rake back his long wavy hair that had fallen forward and continued to write. "I'm also going to make you a Sergeant, for what you did with Brutus and the payroll."

Stand Watie used both hands to lift a long mahogany case up from behind the desk. The warm rich flavor of the reddish-brown wood conquered the tent's interior.

"Paper and ribbons," the old Chief turned Colonel said, "are not enough." He opened the lid to reveal a rifle slumbering on a plush red-black velvet bed. It lay muzzle to butt, left to right, mindful of the fourteen inch Davidson telescopic sight which ran along the left side of the rifle. It had an iron sight graduated out to 1,200 yards that sat atop the barrel, wordlessly revealing an accuracy seven times that of a musket. The steel was married to an age-old walnut tree that had died giving birth to the stock. To a warrior, a soldier or a rifleman, it was simply wondrous.

Designed by Sir Joseph Whitworth and imported from England in the belly of a dull gray steam sloop. With the aid of a low cloud bank, a favorable tide and anthracite coal, the little blockade runner was able to slip past the Union's Goliath of a navy that laired about the South's inlets and waterways.

"Richmond said that I was to have a shooting competition for that rifle, to put fire in the men's spirit," Pike said. "If anyone asks, I'll claim you stole it."

He went back to his writing. "For what you've done in these last three days, I am truly grateful," Pike went on, "but to retain my command, I must reconcile Colonel Drew and his men."

The General stood up. "Sergeant Morgan Black of the Second Cherokee Mounted Rifles, I find you guilty of being absent from camp without leave from the eighth of March 'til the tenth of March, eighteen hundred and sixty-two." He used his service revolver as a gavel, striking the table three times.

xXx

It was arranged quickly, so Watie's men couldn't raise up at the horrendous miscarriage of justice and Drew's men couldn't scream for the scant dispensation of it.

Stand Watie walked next to Morgan. His soldier. The boy who had saved the old Chief's life years earlier. The grandson of his good friend. "I owe you again, but this time more than just my life."

The shuffling and scraping of chains against the earth was the only reply.

"That last shot allowed me my honor."

"That last shot," Morgan stated, "pulled to the left."

They took him to the edge of camp. The provost guards, made

up entirely of Texans, pulled the chains tight between two weathered oaks. Not one of the men were there by choice. A few were full-fledged Indian fighters before this unpleasantness, but they were mostly practical. War has a way of corn-holing everyone without the need of any volunteers.

Instead of the telescope, the gray peacock held a cat-of-nine-tails ready for the General.

Pike left it in the lieutenant's outstretched hand. Albert glanced at Stand Watie, then the Texans and finally back to the young officer.

The young officer understood, developed an intense interest in his boots and started to tremble.

"Brutus."

"Yes Sir?" He said as he removed his straw hat and worked the brim.

Pike reached for one of Brutus' hands, turned it palm up and set the lash into it.

"I can't do this."

"Brutus, you have to," Albert said softly. "If any Indian did this, I'd start an eight hundred man feud. If any Texan did this, both Cherokee factions and all the other Indians would take offense."

The man given the name "Brutus" wasn't highly educated, but he was clever and sharp as a lawyer's tongue. Plus all the years at Albert Pike's considerable side had taught him well.

"You want me to whip this man 'cause he helped you and saved your best man. And you only caught him 'cause he saved your gold?"

"Because it preserves the balance of my command."

"And it's a mystery to you that you're losing this here war?"

"I am not asking about your opinion," Pike said. His rigid tone made it clear that he would abide no more delay to his authority.

Brutus stepped up and to a side, into the same position that others had taken with him, in the feet-wide stance that he'd been forced to watch others take in preparation of landing the first blow.

"Mister, my hand's a'doin' what I don't have the courage to say 'No' to." His resounding baritone didn't betray any of his misgivings. "I reckon you'll kill me later for this?"

Silence answered him. Before the awkward quiet went very far, Pike affected to clear his throat.

Brutus gave a prayer up to his most heavenly father and raised back the lash.

Chapter VI

Steel vs. Steel

The batwing doors exploded inward as Buck stormed into the hotel. He slammed his hands on the counter top. "Where is he?"

"Who?"

Buck grabbed Enos by his cravat. "Don't play dumb. The sack-of-shit that murdered my little brother."

He squirmed for air and pointed towards the double doors.

Buck looked in the direction Enos had pointed and let go of the helpless man.

The clerk was caught off guard with the unexpected release. His want of air made it simply worse. The fall went harsh.

Buck stayed at the counter, the clerk all but forgotten, as he pulled a thumbstall from his pants pocket. It was basically a one-fingered, deerskin glove that an artillery crewman wore to cover the vent hole as another swabbed the cannon tube. It served no practical purpose to wear now. A ritual that he had done dozens of times, before stomping a lifetime of pain into someone. Buck's breath deepened as he cinched it down tight on his thumb and laced it about his wrist. Now he was ready.

Buck never looked back. Although he had been an artilleryman for Jeff Davis, he charged through the doors as well as any strawfoot volunteer who had never seen the elephant. He slowed as his eyes hunted about.

Sara Mae was en route to the trouble when the trouble met her. "I don't want any problems in here, you understand?"

He looked over the top of the smallish lady and laid eyes upon the assassin.

The half-breed bastard sat away from the other patrons, peacefully eating. He even had the gall to wear the uniform of a Confederate three-striper.

Sara Mae went on, but Buck lost interest. His arm brushed her aside with the same motion he'd use to knock dust off a slicker. Buck stood in front of the stranger. His hunt complete. Only a small table stood between them.

The man kept to his meal. Casual. Not even a glance up from his plate.

Buck was eager for this part. He'd done this kind of thing more times than anyone could count. But no one had ever dared ignore him before. Hell was about to cut loose and this stranger paid it no heed. He was either dead stupid or more foolish than a tenderfoot on the back of a riled up Brahma. Beating a half-wit ought to be fun.

"I came here to see the low-life back shooter that done killed my little brother," Buck said in a voice for all to hear. He looked about, reveling in their fear.

"No you didn't."

The stranger's calm words were strange to Buck. He had always rode and raked anyone who got in his way. Those who squared off against him got stomped like a three legged coon hound, or they'd tuck tail and run.

"What?"

"You came here to goad me into a fight."

Buck puzzled. He had to mull over the other man's words until it dawned on him. The stranger was trying to use words to crawl his way out of getting his ass whooped. Yellow. He leaned forward and swiped the table bare. The half-breed looked foolish to Buck, left with just an eating knife and a fork full of pie.

"You have insulted me. I am used to that. You have insulted a lady," Morgan said as he casually pointed towards Sara Mae with his fork. "She runs a business, so she's used to that also." He turned his full attention on the massive bully.

"But the pie is ruined. Apologize."

It was as if the stranger was speaking in tongues, so foreign was it to hear anyone mock a Hertzig. Least of all while seated in his shadow.

Sara Mae covered a grin with her hand. Other customers started to laugh outright.

Buck tried to intimidate the room with a half-mad bestial glare. He focused back on the stranger and opened his mouth to speak.

"Not to me," Morgan clarified, "to the pie."

Buck's face turned sour. He sure wasn't used to folks making fun of him. His immense size only made him look all the more thickheaded. It was well known that the only thing bigger than Buckley Tobias Hertzig was his temper. The hoots and howls from customers merely served to stoke the inferno that consumed him. Buck replied the only way he knew how, with the ivory handled Bowie knife sheathed in his boot.

The stranger was ready for Buck's play. His arm shot upwards as the eating knife did a half roll in the palm of his hand. The tired uniform sleeve snapped as the arm and knife point changed directions. Steel raced steel.

The Bowie knife's run was cut short as Buck bellowed in bloodlust and pain. Buck's off-hand was pegged solid to the table. His eyes widened and his nostrils flared like a wounded bull. Dimly, Buck realized that he was outmatched. He had never seen such speed and deadly precision.

Through the agony, Buck cut loose a plan born out of desperation. His enemy's weapon was now stuck. Useless. He grabbed for the fighting knife with his one still-good hand.

The Indian's instincts took over. Steel flickered and the heavy Bowie clattered along the floor. Buck was stuffed with disbelief. His off-hand had joined the table, courtesy of the stranger's fork.

Buck was not through yet, but at a loss for what to do. Pain destroyed reason. He bit down on the fork and ripped his hand loose. It was a pitiful sight as he tried to work the knife free. A headlong rush of tears, the quavering sounds of a freshly-castrated bull mixed in with cuss words that would force Old Scratch himself to cover his ears and blush.

The stranger stood and moved from behind the table. Buck broke off his work. He could saddle-up no defense against the man who stood above him. The man whom he'd just tried to kill. He toed a lump of pie in front of Buck.

"Apologize."

"You go straight to Hell."

Buck's jaw broke with a dreadful sound as the stranger landed a crushing blow. He dropped like a man cut from a hangman's rope, collapsing the table as it followed the still pinned hand.

Sara Mae watched in complete disbelief as this quiet man stepped over Buck's unconscious frame and resettled at a nearby table.

"Excuse me, Ma'am. I'd be indebted to you if I could have a second piece of your fine peach cobbler."

She looked down at the broken husk of the most fearsome and brutal man she'd ever known. "Anything you want."

"Your word on that?"

"You have my word."

"Then I'd like two pieces."

Sara Mae beamed.

"Brought to my room."

Her smile wavered.

"By you."

Sara took a seat across from the stranger without asking, without thinking. Her mind preoccupied with the dangers that she'd have to face in the ensuing fallout. The whole event played over in her head until she blushed all over. Two pieces.

Coffee was brought. So was the doctor.

Dennis Geraint was never much of a saw-bones. Time had gnarled him up to where his outside matched his demeanor.

The Doc removed the knife and bandaged Buck best he could. He wrapped both the bloody utensils in linen and placed them next to Sara Mae's cup. By evening the next day, he figured, they would join the dozens of other bric-a-brac, knick-knacks, curios and what-nots that Sara Mae displayed throughout the Ambrose.

There was the snake-shaped stick that had made old widow Sellars find religion and had the Giles boy hopping out of town on his one good leg. And the late Mrs. Beel's prized frying pan. And a sword that hung from a thin hemp line. It was as worthless as a bushel of farts in a twister. Fine steel, with an unsharpened edge and made for garnish. It was one way to make an Army musician look like he's ready for war, fiddle and all.

Dozens of items were fixed about. All held a story. A kind of hodgepodge chronicle of local events that added a warm and inviting atmosphere to Sara's place.

To have Buck outthought, outflanked and knocked out was what spectators later claimed to be a simple chore for the man who took six men earlier that same day.

Mounting the Major's oldest son's humiliation up on the Ambrose's wall would be a grand insult. Major Hertzig would not tolerate such defiance. It could only end in fire and death.

It took eight hard-pressed men to lug the sack weight of bully away. The whole thing was done in a mournful silence. Not out of respect for Buck, but for what they feared would happen next to Sara.

Sara Mae waited until the last customer had left. "What do you think you're pulling?"

"You gave your word."

"You know that's not what I meant."

His composure was unnerving. As if his word was law and she'd....

"You gave your word."

"Ok. I apologize for the way I treated you when you first came to my hotel. I was wrong, but not for the reasons you think. If I let just anyone into here, I'd be burned out within a week."

He looked at her as if all that had just come out was air.

"I can't figure you out at all," Sara Mae said with a tired sigh, "but you'll probably be the death of me."

The mixed blood did not swallow the bait to change the subject. He got up, tipped his hat and walked towards his room.

"You think that you can just come in here, give the town bully a thrashing and I'll...I'll have one of the girls from the Four Bits bring you the pie."

He stopped, turned and went back to where she sat. The back of her chair faced him so when he got close, she turned and sipped from her coffee, as if he was no longer there.

She felt the warmth of his soft breath caress her neck from the edge of her collar bone to settle behind her ear.

"I do not want a *Four Bit* piece of pie," he whispered. "I desire a special piece of pie. One that can not be bought, but only freely given. One that would most certainly be treasured."

Sara Mae took in a deep breath and only let it slowly slide from between her lips. She whispered without daring a glance, "I'll be up shortly with your pie."

CHAPTER VII

THE HERALD & THE PIT

J. D. Taylor planned to start out for the Major's place at first light. He wanted to give the undertaker a chance to plug up both sides of Toby's head before stuffing him into the finest coffin-box Calvary could provide. But all the paraffin wax in the world wouldn't ease the pain of a child's death.

With Buck getting thrashed, J. D.'s plan galloped straightaway into the crapper. In the Sheriff's experience, the night has a powerful draw for torches and vigilantes. The Major kept a crew for just such a thing. His sugar plantation's gain was borne on the backs of slaves before the war. Now the same labor was done by Mexicans who had very little say in their own lives. He had no need to hire cowhands. Instead, he took on overseers and toughs. The kind who would get the job done no matter how much the workers had to endure. They were the kind one needs when money or intimidation failed. Just another brand of power. Losers and dregs. Skilled killers all.

J. D. had never locked horns with the Major. Not due to shirking or for any corruption on his part. He just never had a call to.

The Sheriff was a rarity, both born and raised in Calvary. His mother had been a professional ceiling expert, a merchandiser of horizontal refreshment. As he had bloomed up, she had withered out. His mother went from frolicking about a sporting house to plowing in a one room crib and finally lying stiff on a deerskin pelt in an alley. The calamities of Venus, or one of the mercury curatives, took her. Too often those of her trade paid for the wages of sin with their young lives.

John Dante Taylor. His Christian name came from one of his possible fathers and the family name was his mother's legacy. J. D. had no wife or sweetheart. The chaos of his youth he had personally replaced with order. It was his town now. He paid for it with sweat, blood and his childhood. And his mother's disgrace, pain and death.

Before the war, Calvary was a quiet place. There was no boom and bust. It was a steady community, grown up slowly but steadily. Sheriffing was no tougher than a harsh stand or a well placed pistol barrel, and that only every once a piece.

Then the war came. It had exacted a harsh toll on the little town. Several of her sons had marched off to the tune of the Stars and Bars. And were cut down upholding the Southern Cross. Those who could, returned. Some of them missing pieces. Others shattered in different ways.

J. D. had stayed pinned to the star throughout the war. Some doubted his patriotism, but none doubted his courage. He lived for Calvary. And he was its Sheriff.

Reconstruction had flooded into the Lone Star state, but Calvary had weathered the storm virtually unscathed.

The Major had seen to that.

Carpetbaggers swaggered into town like vultures to a fresh kill. Back taxes were assessed that the landowners could not possibly pay. By day, the blue clad occupational troops protected the carpetbaggers as they scuttled in and scavenged what they wanted.

Then they started to vanish. Always at night. It was well known, but never proven, that the Major was behind the disappearances. The rest of the northern skunks decided to move on to easier pickings. Sold what properties that they had gained at pennies on the dollar, for sometimes less than what they themselves had paid. Survival became more important than money.

The Major reluctantly bought every piece of property from them to stave off any further northern interference, then leased it back to the original owner. This was no act of charity. In one form or another, the Major always got his due.

Taylor shared the buckwagon's seat with Pastor Hiram Evander, who slumbered fitfully next to him.

Before the Pastor had settled in Calvary, he went from county to county and walked where Judges feared to tread. In those days, his two companions were the Holy Spirit and a simple wooden staff. Both had protected him. Both he had used to help others find salvation. Back then, his only other belongings were the clothes on his back, the good book that he wielded like a sword and the righteous trumpet of his conviction.

Hiram had entered his forties with a whimper. The flame of his calling had sputtered out like a match floating in a spittoon. It wasn't any flashy instant or any life and death case that had changed him. Faith is belief. And hardships had led him to questions. Angry questions. Hateful questions. So now he went through the motions, treating the pulpit as a business venture rather than a venerated shepherd's post.

Buck sat dangling his legs off the wagon's tail end. He leaned on his brother's casket, moaning with his bandaged head in his bandaged hands for the whole ride.

The Sheriff pulled to a stop at the gates to the Major's property. The sudden halt awoke the preacher and did wonders for Buck's jawbone.

The grillwork above the plantation's entranceway held the property's mark. A "9" within a ring. The "Circle Nine." It was the largest spread in the county and with topnotch soil for raising sugar.

Past the gates it was a straight shot to the Hertzig ranch. Old World cobblestones lined the way from gate to house. A fine pecan orchard, branches intertwining above the path, loomed like mute centurions standing their post.

Beams of lemony moonlight speared through the overhead canopy, illuminating the cave-like path that led to the Major's.

The spread was breathtaking. It rivaled those of antebellum plantations of the Old Dominion and the Carolinas. The main house was a thick, straight-angled, two-story affair made of unpainted brick.

The white columned portico wrapped about the entire mansion, like a Roman temple and barracks merged into one grand building. Jeffersonian classicism at its finest.

At the mansion's front, the road coiled back on itself, circling a small island of grass. A flagpole, tall as three men, was stationed behind a brass cannon. The field piece was a Confederate standard 12-pounder. A Napoleon. It had retired along with the Major from the late unpleasantness. Now it sat, empty, defending the past. Silent, except for the fourth of July and twelfth of April. Both anniversaries of Independence. One for the red, white and blue. While the other was for the day that the tyrant's blue was torn asunder and replaced with freedom's gray.

Solid cannon shot was stacked four high, forming little pyramids at the four compass points about the gun-howitzer. A dozen more circled about on short posts. Each post-top was scooped out so a cannon ball could roost on it.

These were different. They were hollow. In time of war, they would have had iron balls and gunpowder inside, capped with a fuse plug. The war was over, except for the remorse, and these twelve had been all gussied up since the peace. Half of them had been dipped in silver and the rest in gold. They alternated from one precious metal to the other as they circled around the cannon.

A young man, in his late teens and darkened from his Aztec and Spanish ancestry, hurried forward before they had come to a stop. He was dressed as a house servant, down to the white cotton gloves and tails.

"You wanna go out back. I take care of your horses and everything," the Mexican said, looking far too happy for the late hour. He helped them with the reins and held one glove, palm heavenward, in front of the Clergyman.

"I'm a man of God," Hiram said as he went past, giving decent care to straighten down his Sunday duds.

The servant replied in Spanish. It was bitter, cutting and crude, but his grin remained fresh.

Taylor shared in the sarcasm, without saying a word. Being Sheriff had taught him what books hadn't. He well understood the Pastor.

And the piece of truth that lay buried in the young Mexican's reply. But it wasn't his place to interfere.

Buck went inside, leaving the Sheriff, the Pastor and Toby to the chilled darkness.

They left the corpse in the wagon without complaint.

"Guess we'll go out back then."

The Lawman and Bible-thumper ventured around the house, through brick-lined gardens and well groomed lands. The way was well-lit by the full moon, which was a jaundicy yellow, as if it had been boiled in old-wax and cadaver lard.

The earth gradually descended and led to a small lake, formed from a horseshoe tributary that fed into the Brazos river. In its twisting it had become cut-off, stagnant and still as death.

They could see a red glow that flickered about the cottonwoods and willows that ringed the man-made island near the lake's center. They smelled the bonfires eating away at good wood, could almost taste the sugar from the mill and the vapors from the lake.

The island itself was built up on a shoal with the Major's money and the lives of several workers. As a Texas Ranger, Johannes Hertzig had been taught that killing bean-eaters, redskins and niggers didn't count.

A jetty waited for them at the water's edge. Empty, except for an old ship's bell that hung from an rusty arch at the plankway's threshold.

The Sheriff rang the bell.

"I... think we should go back now," the man of the cloth said.

It was not long before a small barge emerged from the island's reed wall. The moonlight turned the plants a dire gray and the lake into a place that could fuel nightmares.

The lake held the decaying rattons and other filth from years of sugar production. The unsettling odors coming off the stale waters only added flavor to the Pastor's misgivings.

A former slave poled to the landing. He was a leftover from the Emancipation. Too old to leave. Too hopeless to care. Skinny as a shroud. His skin seemed to be made of ash, in complexion and texture, chafing off in ugly patches that became stuck in his matted straggle of a wisp-thin, grease-white beard. His eyes glared from within a grimy cowl and cloak, both knotted together from castoffs and rags. He seemed formless. A shade clutching a stick.

Without a word, they started across the onyx-colored waters.

Chapter VIII

Passion & Murder

Sara Mae padded down the hall. In her stockinged feet she was as quiet as she was curious.

Room seven.

Two pieces.

She blushed.

It had been a few hours since all the action downstairs had ended. The Sheriff had swung by. "Just checking on things." He asked a few questions, but Sara could plainly see that her answers were already expected. He said nothing about why she had allowed a half-breed to have a room or a meal in the main room, or why there was a crossed fork and knife newly-tacked on the wall next to where Buck tried to ride roughshod over another stranger.

"Tell him that I need to see him first thing tomorrow," J. D. had said.

Sara's musings spilled away when she realized that she stood in front of number seven. She caught her breath, ran a hand over her hair and made one final check that everything was tucked, buttoned or straight. Both cheeks received a good firm pinch for coloring.

Her calico dress still smelled of cedar and rose petals from being stowed away. It was her favorite. Union blue and white that time had stripped the bright off. Underneath the long skirt were a pair of the deepest blue-silk pantaloons. They had seen service when her husband returned from the war. Sara was a rock-ribbed Virginian, and her unreturned love had torn her up like a loser in a straight razor duel.

Now she wore her Union dress, for the Confederate stranger, like a flag raised high up atop a fieldwork after the first salvo had been fired.

Sara wondered if she should tap lightly, leave the plate and tell him that she tried. Or maybe throw open the door and demand his intentions? Two pieces? Indeed!

As she stood there, still deciding, the door opened.

"Please, come in."

Sara looked down both sides of the hallway, assuring herself that no one would know, before she entered.

The stranger shut the door to one awkward moment just to stand in the middle of the next, as she thrust the pie towards him.

"Here, sit down." He motioned to the foot of the bed, while he took up the brass-railed headboard.

"No. It would not be proper."

Morgan held his first answer between his teeth, then said in a gentle manner. "I will not bite. I promise."

"I said "No."

"How can you enjoy some pie, standing there with that look on your face?"

Sara was frustrated. She did not like this man. His calm strength. The subtle smile that sprang to his face every time she talked to him. Or that the same damned smile kept trying to gain her lips. No, she would not like this man!

She sat down, but at the foot of the bed, and she put the cobbler down like a fence-line between them.

"You're nothing like my husband was."

"The man who left you for a working girl?"

His words burned. But Sara knew that he was right. He had seen the spike that she had locked-up and hidden, that she twisted herself about every day with questions of why, or self-doubt, or what to do now? At night, it was worse, as she wept, not for herself, but for their fatherless son.

"You can't possibly know anything about me."

"Yes, I do. He told me about you," he said softly. "And then you told me."

"What? What are you talking about?"

Morgan leaned over and pulled a bundled handful of letters from his pommelbags.

She could not be sure, but it looked as if he had every piece of mail that she had sent to Phillip, her husband. They were personal. And the contents ranged from a lock of Alex's hair to Sara's outpourings of despair. She felt soiled, as though she should slap him, but she wouldn't. Not yet anyway.

"You have your pie. Two pieces. You can stay the night, but in the morning you're going to leave," Sara said, fighting to retain her composure. "And never set foot inside my place again."

xXx

The intruder slipped into Mrs. Hertzig's hotel room as quiet as a thought. Quiet continued as the ghost-like predator shut the door, eyes fixed on the slumbering mother of four. The distance between them was closed at a creep. A custom gold-plated Derringer at the ready.

xXx

"I was to be hanged," Morgan said it as a fact, not ashamed or as a braggart.

Sara Mae had her back to him, doorknob in hand, poised to leave, when his words gave her pause. She turned to listen.

"Your husband was to be hanged also. He was drunk. They had spent all his money. His lady-friend said she was leaving. She fell off a balcony."

He picked up a slice and offered it to her, where it hung.

"So how did you get my letters?"

"Bite."

"The letters?" she said.

"Bite."

Sara waited for the story to continue. He waited also. With a heavy sigh, she reached for the pie.

"No," Morgan smiled. "Bite."

The pie was her mother's and her mother's mother's recipe. Ever since she could remember, Sara had had that exact pie. Probably even before she could walk. But it had been ages since she had truly tasted it. Savored its delicate crust that beautifully mingled with the soft-warmth of the peach filling.

"Prison can make a man hard or can turn a man into something very soft," he continued. "Killing a woman is not manly. So he paid me with your letters to protect him."

"Did you protect him?"

"Right up until he was hanged."

"And they paroled you and you came looking for me?"

"No," Morgan replied. "Bite."

Sara let him feed her.

"I escaped."

She absently chewed, deep in thought, and decided not to ask too much, although she was bursting to know. Like how he had escaped? Or why was he in prison in the first place? Or a hundred other questions that bustled about inside her. No, she'd wait until he wanted to tell her, even if it killed her.

Sara changed the subject, hoping that he wouldn't notice the warmth pouring onto her cheeks. "He must have said something awfully good about me for you to travel all this way to see me."

"No. He said you were short and plain. That you thought too much. Told too many people what was on your mind. And that you were the stubbornest woman ever to walk on the face of the earth."

She was shocked, not that her husband would say such a thing, but that this man would look her straight in the eye and repeat it.

"Then why are you here?"

He presented her with another bite and she leaned into it, like a baby bird waiting to be taken care of. And he smiled.

xXx

Mrs. Hertzig's dream had twisted into a sickness. One filled with images of her dead son and of evil spirits. It kept replaying, and each time she was more desperate to save him. Each time she was only laughed at, with pure contempt at her efforts. The voice came from nowhere and everywhere. All at the same time. Distorted echos blended with mocking laughter. Amplifying the pain-regret-loss of her lifeless baby-boy. The worst of it was that she knew the voice. The man behind her torment. And that the dream was true.

She awoke, covered in sweat, afraid to move. The pillow's softness and the blanket's warmth reassured her. Yes, she knew that Toby had gone to Heaven, but tomorrow would be another day, and she knew that her other children would still need her.

A pillow fell gently upon her face as the Derringer's hammer was cocked back with a quiet snap that roared in Mrs. Hertzig's ears.

xXx

Morgan was a soldier's soldier. Since his early childhood, warfare and death had been his constant companions. But instead of losing its meaning, life became all the more precious to him, and lovemaking was the ultimate celebration of life. He expressed it with an unremitting intensity. His passion was undeniable. It showed in his every touch. His every move. His lips adored her in ways that no confessional could ever make right.

And she had never needed anything more.

They shared their breath as they became one.

Sara, lost in his arms, had found her bliss. The kind an innocent girl believes in, yet a woman rarely finds. She felt warm and safe. Wrung out, yet wishing it would go on and on without end. Her body continued thrashing as she drifted on a glorious bed of clouds.

For the first time since her husband had left, she was able to see past the anger. Past the feelings of betrayal.

Philip had fiddled the war away. A musician of limited ability. His real skill was in the art of hogwash. Women would swoon and

Generals would feel even more like gods after he had stuffed their ears with honey.

Her husband had taken his bridal pleasures in the shortest fashion possible. And it had only grown worse throughout the war. On the rare occasion he'd show up on leave, he was more interested in her skills as a laundress than those of a loving wife. When the guns of war became silent, so did their bedroom.

Responsibility chafed Phillip like a horsehair shirt. Their son was born shortly after he went off to war, so it wasn't until afterwards that fatherhood became a millstone about his neck. A child would get in the way of what he felt was his true calling. As a musician, he had learned that the love of two could never be compared to being adored by dozens. Every time he gazed at their bright-eyed gift from God there was dread in his eye.

Then her husband was gone. No warning. No goodbye note. The only thing he left was loneliness and not enough money for the nextday's meal....

She was pulled back to the instant as her world shattered and melted as all thought was replaced with pure sensation. A primal outcry burst forth from some deep unknown place.

The man, whom Sara hadn't even asked his name, had taught her the rebel yell.

CHAPTER IX

BLOODY SPURS & BAD MEN

J. D. and Hiram sat silently as the ferry coursed a short labyrinth hewn through the reeds towards the island.

The Pastor looked as if the voyage had sweated him mightily. His skin paled to the same color as a catfish's underbelly. "What do you call this place?"

"Dis?" Said the glum-faced, Methuselah-old boatman. "Dis was created by de Mayjor. No udder name be needed."

No escort awaited them, but the only wooded pathway had torches fairly regular along the way. The noises were distinct now. What had sounded like a gigantic, hungry, growling dragon slowly awakening from a long held slumber had unfolded into the excited cheers and curses of men.

As they neared the island's center, they could make out the outline of an immense circular structure. Cotton bales, five hundred pounds each, were piled nine high to make up the outside perimeter.

The trail lead them directly to a tunnel opening that burrowed itself into the mountainous construct.

A Mastiff, ugly as he was fierce, was chained to a half buried ship's anchor to one side of the opening. A massive, imposing, slobbering, snorting, deadly, fart-filled beast of Herculean strength. Generations of killing had been bred into him, transforming his spirit into a machine of primal destruction. No amount of chain or steel could make a man feel safe in his presence.

The tunnel was darker than Satan's heart. Prudent. The last thing someone needs when surrounded by tons of cotton is fire. It had no branches or turns. A straight, temperate descent, until they emerged.

Once inside, torches were set about casting a hellishly dancing light about the vast coliseum. The cotton bales were stacked one less high than the outer ring progressively, funneling a tiered seating arrangement down towards the arena floor. The last was still three bales tall, nearly twelve feet above the arena sand. From amidst the cotton were wooden pillars that ran upwards, supporting a simple roof, grayish and without detail in the smoke and smells that it trapped.

The walls around the sand were arranged in an odd egg-shaped fashion, with a massive wrought iron post centered in the wider end. An oversized double door of the same iron make was located in the far end of the arena's wall, directly opposite the post. The doors and the field itself were framed in flame-blackened timbers, some deeply scored by claw or horn.

Blood sports. Where packs of dogs fought against each other or set against a single bull or bear. The combinations were only limited by the spectacle of death and gambling's seduction.

But tonight's festivities revolved around a Main. Most cockpits were either circular or square, but this one had been readied at the narrow end of the larger arena, causing it to have five sides. A large iron cauldron held fire at each corner, flickering strange shadows about.

The screams and shouts died down and were shortly replaced by catcalls and other sounds of disapproval. The assembled crowd lived for fast, brutal action and this was becoming a drag fight.

They went down a temporary staircase that took them onto the sand, circled about the fight, and through the ever-changing infernal stench that ranged from fresh blood and rot to burning strips of dried orange peels. To Hiram, the whole of it was offensive, like a two-bit whore splashed with five dollars of snake-oil perfume. J. D. barely noticed. There were worse things than a few unpleasant smells.

The runaway gamecock got last count and the match was over. The Irish Gilder's spirit had broken along with his wing.

J. D. was surprised to see Mr. Franks wearing an ankle length, blood stained, leather apron and refereeing the fights.

They could see the Major clearly now, perched upon a throne that stood on the closest tier to the sand. The throne itself was rough cut from a singe bale of cotton and a lion's pelt kept the white fibers from sticking to Mr. Hertzig.

He loomed over the spectacle, omniscient. A Roman Centurion who had hacked his way into a Senatorial seat. Dignified to the point of arrogance. No one in this part of Texas was half as powerful. He knew it. And it showed.

Thirty years ago, in Georgia, Johannes had been a Militia Captain during the removal of the Savage. After that, as a Texas Ranger, he fought against Mexes and Heathen alike. Most recently, he had been a Confederate Major until he resigned his commission and came back to Calvary in '63. The last rank stuck to him like molasses to fur. Those who knew him called him by his former rank with varying amounts of respect and fear. But none who knew him called him by his surname any longer. Johannes Hertzig had become "the Major."

The next two gamecocks were being weighed when the Pastor and Sheriff finally reached their destination. The roosters were within two ounces of each other and ready to kill.

The Major was never more his title than at that very moment, altogether dudded-up in a deepest grey officer's double breasted frock coat. The two rows of buttons were of solid gold and the lapels were folded open to reveal the red folds of his inner tunic. A small officer's cape, flipped back on his shoulders, revealed a blood-red silk brocade lining. A wine colored sash wrapped twice about his waist, and thigh length Dragoon boots, polished to the ideal of perfection, completed the outfit.

The uniform was of a quality that the Major never possessed during the war, but it lacked a headpiece. No kepi, slouch or even the stiff-felted Jeff Davis, all plumed and tasseled. The Major wore nothing but a bright red kerchief, like the pirates of old, since before he stepped on Texas soil. He wore it every day and at all times. And had never been seen without it.

At his side was a sword of standard length and plain as stale hardtack. So common in appearance that it looked out of place among all the finery.

He was built like a grizzly. Thick with muscle and backbone. With a jaw set square as a Freemason's loyalty. His saber-gray hair curled about his shoulders, with his well groomed moustache and full beard ending in a decisive point.

He was looking down at them, since the end of the cockfight they had his full attention.

Hiram attempted to clear his throat and swab off his forehead with his already moist handkerchief. "I... ah... think that the Sheriff has something to tell you." He looked to J. D. with an unspoken plea.

"Jesus, Hiram, you don't look like you're faring well?" the Major said, the caliber of his voice loaded with concern. "You look as if somebody died."

J. D. glanced over and saw that the Pastor was aging by the second. "Franks already told you about what happened?"

The Major brought his trigger finger to his lips and then aimed it at the pit behind them. "The next fight is just about to start."

The pitters circled about inside the ring, showing off their cocks for all to see. It was as formalized as any gentlemen's duel.

The Major's champion was a Warhorse with the finest of inbred blood purging all weakness from his veins.

The challenger was an Eslin Red Horse. Worthy, but it hadn't been born yet. It had fought its way out of the egg. Penwalked, flirted and conditioned for the day it would be heeled and pitted. But a gamecock wasn't born until it had blood on its spurs.

Only the foolish, and then only at extravagantly favorable odds, wagered on the newcomer. "You should bet on that one Preacher."

"Bill your cocks!" Franks commanded.

Still held, the antagonists flared as their handlers brought them together inside the score lines. Beaks clashed, raising hackles and their natural killing spirit.

"What odds will you give?" J. D. asked.

"Thirty to one," the Major fired back without the slightest hesitation.

"Twenty dollars?"

"Done!" The Major slapped his knee in triumph. "This is getting interesting now, by God."

"Get ready."

For five measured seconds the crowd froze.

Emboldened by the Major's spirits, the Pastor tried to add his condolences for the loss of a son. He was cut off before a single note left his throat by one simple gesture from the Major.

"Pit!"

They crashed into each other, man-shoulder high, parting low and shuffling fast. Feathers flew and colors danced as they tore about the pit.

The audience exploded. Blood was what they had come for.

The first pitting was as long as it was glorious. Both gave as good as they got, both dripping gore, and neither lost any ground.

"Handle!"

Both pitters picked up their birds and immediately started stroking and feeling, assessing the damage and how much quiver was still untapped.

"Hungry?"

They both turned to the Major.

"I have some batter cakes."

"No thanks." Hiram stared out over the crowd. "I'm not feeling good."

The Sheriff accepted and was thankful for the gut-stuffers.

"Pit!"

The next one was over when they hit the ground, the Major's Warhorse hung a spur deep. The challenger's choking rattle told of a punctured lung.

Franks pulled out the steel carefully, making dead certain that the spur didn't twist.

The Elsin's handler put his mouth over his gamecock's beak and sucked the blood from his bird's lungs. Spat. And was ready.

"These preservatives are first-rate," the Sheriff said, "what is it?"

"Pomegranate."

"Pit!"

They shuffled back and forth. The Warhorse topped the challenger, but got beaten off by a stiff-legged defense. And they cut each other until feathers and blood littered the pit. Beak to beak, they slammed into the walls and still they kept at it. Then it was over. The Warhorse lay dead. A single shot to the brain.

It was one of those "Ah, shit" victories. What the ancient Romans would've called a Pyrrhic victory. The challenger did not live long enough to be separated from the Major's dead champion.

The Pastor watched the flurry as bets were settled amid the rambunctious audience.

"Cursed be to Mammon."

The Major finished counting out the six hundred he had just lost, plus his best fighting cock. And now this dig.

"Oh come now, Pastor, I never heard you utter one curse as it filled your pockets."

"The collection plate is to do God's work."

"Oh? I'm sorry. I was speaking of the strongbox you keep in the bank."

The Pastor replied the best he could, with profound embarrassment and a troubled silence.

They rode more than half way back to Calvary without speaking.

"Here," J. D. said, handing a wad of greenbacks to the Pastor.

"No, thank you," Hiram dismissed the offer. "It wouldn't be right."

The Sheriff shrugged his shoulders and stuck the money back inside his vest.

"I thought you were going to ask the Major a bunch of questions?"

"No," Taylor replied. "I said I had a bunch of questions."

"Well, why didn't you ask him any?"

"He wouldn't have answered them straightaways. But he'd have known what I was figuring at." J. D. pulled a bottle from beneath the seat. "Anyhow, some of them were answered and some new ones cropped up."

"Like what?"

"Like were those gamecocks dangerous enough for the Major to throw up hundreds, maybe thousands, of cotton bales around them? Mr. Franks is one of the few men as good with his gun as he is vicious. He'd nail the baby Jesus to the cross if hired to. No hired gun travels for weeks to judge a chicken match."

"Thanks," the Pastor took a deep pull from the offered rotgut. "Why do you think the Major didn't ask about what happened with the stage?"

"Franks, and probably others, had already filled him in. Plus the Major is a man of strength. Did you really expect him to ask questions that might make him appear weak?"

They went back to silence until they could make out the town from the darkness. The fretful quiet remained even after the spirits were drained.

"What did you think about tonight's events?"

The Pastor thought about it. "I'd say tonight held a lot of revelations."

xXx

Sara had left as dawn broke. Full of guilt, shock and fear. And a terrible longing for more. She had kissed him once before departing, light and tender. She asked for nothing, said not a word and needed no false promises.

It was nearly an hour later when Morgan awoke with a start. A noise from the open window came in that he had heard hundreds of variants of. Sounds of the strong dominating the weak just because they could. Because other weak people would avert their eyes and pretend that nothing bad could happen to those who ignore suffering. Or worse, those that would watch, spectators of misery.

Down on the street, through the morning ground-hugging fog, Morgan saw three men as they taunted, prodded and pushed at a lady. Vultures circling about a dove. She looked pure. Her manner both courtly and helpless. With perfect blaze-red hair and a dress blacker than the Original Sin. But it was the swaddling that she kept turning away from their advances that sent him into a whirlwind of action.

CHAPTER X

THE HORSESHIT WALTZ

Morgan dropped to the street in his longjohns, LeMat at the ready, and rushed after them as they herded her into Isaiah's livery.

The lady's resistance was divided. Her concern for what she held overrode whatever they were about.

Quiet was not an option when the stable door opened grudgingly for him. Inside the livery's dimness, Morgan could make out more than a half dozen men. They crowded about her, grabbing as they laughed and jeered at her. None paid the doorway any mind.

He entered and quickly sidestepped away from the easy target of the backlit entranceway and into the early morning shadows cast by the livery's interior.

She turned, still desperately trying to protect her armload, and somehow she saw the half-naked Indian coming towards her. With a frightened yelp, she bolted. The violence of her reaction sent the cherished bundle flying.

Action overtook thought as Morgan dove, arms extended. He landed with a jolt in a large heap of collected muck. It was apparent that Isaiah had only half finished the morning cleaning when they had descended on his shop.

Morgan was sprawled out, stretched to full length, his fingertips held the baby-swathe.

But something was wrong.

What should have been soft, supple and precious, was solid, odd-shaped, and common. The linen unraveled to reveal the same fake bundle of dynamite that he'd used the day before, less the twine fuse.

Now they had him.

Usually, Longhorn was bone idle. Allergic to anything that even accidentally resembled honest work. But beating a helpless man wasn't honest work. He cast about for something to ease the chore with, spotted a short handled shovel and made for it.

The others knew what they were about, but were thrown off by the presence of a lady. Each knew what she wanted them to do, but they hadn't counted with her standing close enough to taste the bloodshed.

So they stood there and gazed down at their quarry. He was smaller than any of them had imagined. Older too. But even these rawhide and gristle men hadn't expected to see the terrible lattice of scars that only floggings leave behind. There were other scars too. Fearsome ones. From stabs and slashes. Bullets and fire. Part of his right shoulder was permanently tattooed black from a charge of half burnt gunpowder.

The lady laughed. It would have been a splendid thing, light and airy. Modest. Fit for a social event at the Carnegies. Amid the dung-pile and expected brutality, it was a perverse sound.

Morgan burst into action. Still prone, he lashed out with the bundle, landing a vicious backhand to the knee of one on his left. The cheapjack didn't go down, but jumped away from the unexpected attack, knocking into two of his buddies.

A kick landed in the Cherokee's ribs, from the other side. He rolled with it and rolled again.

They started after him.

The roll ended with Morgan on his back. Pistol trained and hammer thumbed back with an audible click. It oozed with filth, but was no less deadly.

They reined in their advance and were struck dumb by the appearance of the revolver, looking like altar boys caught putting tadpoles in the christening stoup.

"Sum bitch," Longhorn said with a graveled voice.

"Gun belts."

Longhorn looked to the others, seeing if they'd drop leather or pull iron. None reckoned that the stranger's trigger finger was any worse than the day before. Holster after holster fell flat.

"Sum bitch."

"Where is Isaiah?"

"Don't know. He wasn't here when we arrived," said the dirtiest of the lot.

Morgan looked past the man's filth. The man was sweating, yet he wasn't breathing hard and had bits of dried upchuck on his cotton shirt and he wore no jacket. A sick man bundles up tight. His illness spoke of opium, the Chinese condition. But the wilted ostrich plume affixed to a grey slouch hat that had died on top of the man's headbone attested to a different history.

"You fought for the Cause?"

The man lit up, "Hell, yeah." He grew with the pride of past achievement and was shocked that this man had recognized him as a veteran. "Rode with Stuart from the start."

"You rode around the Union Army?"

"Oh hell yeah I did!"

"Now you ride around the Dragon?" Morgan asked.

His esteem squirmed away, leaving only the dried spew and memories. Nothing cuts deeper than pure distilled truth.

That's when Morgan saw it. They'd grubbed about in his war-bag and kit, looking for sellables. His spare clothes were tossed willy nilly. A small traveling bag, filled with roller bandages, catgut and bullet-doctoring tools, had been up-assed and rooted about. All of that mattered naught.

They had broken his grandfather's saber.

His grandfather had been a great Cherokee warrior. "Kills-In-Water" was harder than flint and twice as sharp. Once he had been attacked by four Creek warriors while he had "gone to water" to purify himself. He let one limp home to his tribe with the message, "Never desecrate a Cherokee ritual."

Grandfather had lived a balanced life in the middle world. The white man held nothing for him unless he took it while counting coup. His grandfather had risked his life for that sword while fighting with Andy Jackson against the Lobsterbacks at New Orleans.

His grandfather was gone now. So was the sword.

Morgan looked to the former yellow-leg. "You let them do this?"

"No, I was out on picket, waiting for you." The man took his own words as an insult to himself, knowing that he'd been the signalman.

"One at a time, pick up your guns and toss them into the loft."

Longhorn sensed that something had changed. That the Indian wanted their guns altogether done and gone, was bad, real bad, but there wasn't a tinker's damn he could do about it.

Morgan's pistol decided the order in which they submitted.

With restrained grumbling and only one more "Sumbitch," they chucked their iron. They had heard about yesterday and today saw for themselves his speed and cunning. There was no question that this man was prepared to kill faster than a hummingbird's fart.

It came down to the last of them, the poppyhead.

"Ready your gun," Morgan said.

"What?"

"Ready your gun."

"I can't..." He glanced at his pack-mates and back to the half-naked Indian. "I use opium. To kill the pain. I keep my gun empty. So I don't hurt nobody."

Some of his "friends" chuckled at this. The others laughed outright. But not Morgan.

The half-breed walked up, uncocked his pistol and placed it firmly into the user's hand.

"Then use mine."

"What?"

"You have a choice. You can keep your buddies from attacking me," Morgan said, "or you can shoot me in the back."

"What's this about?"

"You."

"What if I do nothing?"

"Then you stay as you are." Morgan turned and walked towards the red haired "lady."

This man didn't want choices. He was happy in his narcotic oblivion. But that was bullshit and he knew it. A lie that became harder and harder for him to believe, but the more he used, the less he cared for the truth. The easiest fool to trick was himself, when an honest look in the mirror seemed too hurtful to swallow.

He looked down at the pistol and was shocked. It was the same type of contraptionous pistol that General Stuart himself had used. It was a massive affair that held nine shots in a cylinder and pivoted around an 18-bore shotgun barrel that held a load of grapeshot. It was a rarity. And proclaimed its owner as an unreconstructed Confederate.

Longhorn laughed and picked up the shovel. Another sat down on a rail, rubbing his shin. The others were tethered to Longhorn's lead.

"Drop it."

Longhorn turned and looked in disbelief. The monstrous pistol was aimed at him again. "You're not man enough to use that hogleg, Jack."

"I was once," Jack said. He reached up, smoothed the rat-tailed ostrich plume with his free hand and smiled for the first time in years. "Are you willing to bet your life that I ain't now?"

Longhorn thought about it. "Sumbitch." The shovel was cast aside.

Morgan pulled up in front of the genteel woman, affected to tip his hat that wasn't there and said, "Ma'am."

The lady looked like she'd sucked the yellow off a barrel of lemons. She saw a look of whimsy in his face. "You find this amusing?"

"Yes."

"Do you have any idea of who I am?"

"The lady who just tried to have me hurt?"

His words vexed her. She was so comfortably used to men running from her displeasure. "I am Justine. Justine *Hertzig*." The Major's daughter expected a frightened man to recoil and fall all over himself apologizing. She was sorely disappointed.

"These men will kill you if you lay a single finger on me," she motioned towards Longhorn and the others.

The man, who'd just rolled around in horseshit, glanced down at her locket. It was a beautiful piece. Silver. With her father's image carved into it. Something dark passed over his face that Justine couldn't understand.

"Maybe. But I live now."

"I don't know what you expect, but you aren't going to just waltz your way out of here alive."

"There are easier ways to catch a man's eye."

Her open palm flew in response, but Morgan caught her in mid-slap, as casually as a father would his misbehaving child. He pulled her close and wrapped his right arm about her waist, leaving a small space between her curvaceous dignity and his shit-covered bare chest.

She knew the position. "I will not!"

"Ladies are respectful. Children are rude," Morgan said in an emotionless voice. "Ladies dance. Children get spanked."

"You would not dare," she proclaimed. Each word came out one at a time to add weight to her refusal. She knew men. With a word, or a bat of an eyelash, they were hers. Married or single, sinner or saint, it didn't matter. Until now. This man was giving her two choices. No negotiation. No compromise.

He led as they began to dance. His rhythm and timing were consistent and expressed a fairytale-like quality. His footwork had no beginning or end, a flow of polished motion.

She followed his lead. Not that she wanted to. It took her a moment to realize why. It was fear. In her heart, she knew this man would carry out whatever he said. Dance or a spanking. One or the other. The idea of being thrown over this man's lap, her hoop skirt pitched over her head and his rough powerful hand crashing down upon her....

"I say you are no proper gentleman!" Justine referred to his manners, for nothing could change what he was in her mind.

"A proper gentleman would still be on the floor."

He set a slow tempo, rotating a quarter turn counter-clockwise every three steps, as they made their way about the livery.

"This is completely absurd."

"I agree."

"You agree?"

"Yes. It is absurd to lure a man from his bed and into a pile of horseshit."

She gave up trying. It was pointless. This red-skinned barbarian was just too uneducated to comprehend how ludicrous this entire situation was. She'd planned the ambush well. And she'd have curried her father's favor. Now her tactics were not only defeated, but had turned it into something ridiculous, worst of all, with her help. Every moment that passed, her hatred snowballed.

Morgan lifted his left hand, still holding her slapper. His right guided her into a slow spin towards him and under their upraised arms. She completed the spin, facing him at arms length. Morgan released her. She stood in the same spot where they had started.

"May I have my handbag so I can leave now?" She pointed to where it lay on top of a stall railing. It was a rich burgundy affair, dainty in size.

Morgan picked it up. Not like a lady would, by the clasp, but as a man grabs an apple off a tree. He made to hand it to her, stopped, felt its contents, smiled and tossed it up into the loft.

"Someday, I'm going to shoot you," Justine said in a voice that was both strained and seductive.

"That day, you will no longer be a *proper* lady."

She made a "humpf" sound and her face suckled lemons once more.

Jack handed the loaned pistol back to Morgan. "Thank you," he said and turned to Longhorn. "Tell the Major I quit."

"You're yeller."

"Nope. Just been running away from myself. I'm here now. Best you remember that before ever speaking to me again."

"You respect this Sumbitch for what he just done?"

"Nope." Jack cinched up his backbone a notch, "I respect him for what he didn't do."

That made no sense to Longhorn, and he couldn't let it lie the way it stood.

"You think it right? The way he jes grabbed the Major's daughter and forced her to do a two-step?"

"Nope," Jack smiled broadly. "It was a *Waltz*."

CHAPTER XI

LOVE & A MASSACRE

16ᵗʰ of July, 1839. About half a mile from Neches in the Republic of Texas. Two regiments of Militia and Rangers were in their second day of battle against the Cherokee and members of more than a dozen other tribes.

Mirabeau Bonaparte Lamar, the Republic's second president and Sam Houston's successor, had instituted his policy of extermination and removal of the Red Man. Tried, found guilty and sentenced to death in the single stroke of a pen.

Chief Diwa-li, known by the White-man as Chief Bowles or just "The Bowl," had already ordered the women and children to flee North in an attempt to save them, for mercy was not included in the decree.

Morgan Black had stood shoulder-to-shoulder with the other warriors the day before. He had fought bravely, and his ability with a rifle was talked about on both sides that night. Morgan had killed his first man, but had hardly noticed as he began to reload before the man slid from the saddle. His grandfather had taught him well. The boy was not yet ten years old.

Chief John Bowles himself came that night to see Morgan, his mother and his baby sister, Catherine. The eighty-three year old leader praised Morgan's mother for raising such a fine young man. Then he spoke to the boy.

"You were sent to join us by Stand Watie. In the letter you brought with you he asked me to look after your family."

Morgan waited for him to continue.

The Bowl drew his sword and placed it in the youth's hands. It was a standard, United States Army-issue, saber. No engraved platitudes or plated garnish. The cooking fire's reflection struggled to dance along the unpolished blade.

"It was given to me by Sam Houston, but it has grown into a symbol to our people," the Chief said. In his voice and in his actions, it was plain to see the pure reverence that the venerated old Cherokee held for the sword.

"Tomorrow, I can't wield it and look after your family."

Morgan looked up from the sword. "What would you have me do?"

The next morning found the boy using his rifle to break trail through the marshy thickets. His mother gave Catherine her milk, making it harder to keep up.

He was covered in a slew of cuts, bites and bruises from the effort, but he hurried onward. Their escape had been cut off several times and they were forced to circle back as small and bloody skirmishes broke out all around them.

The boy did not take part in the main battle this day.

Diwa-li had asked him to escort his family to safety and for his musket flints. The Texans had captured their only major supply the day before, so his rifle was only dangerous to the brush blocking their way.

Morgan smashed through to a grassy clearing and came to a dead stop. They could see a hundred-odd Cherokee warriors, broken and scattered about where they had fallen. He could see Chief Bowles atop his fine white-blazed Sorrel, wearing a black military hat from a bygone age and swinging his sword in defiance. The great Chief and a few others, had stayed behind after the battle was lost, to buy time with their lives.

Finally, Diwa-li's voice boomed out the order to retreat. He wheeled his mount and started to leave the field as several musket shots slammed into his red-brown horse. The Bowl was thrown clear and only slowly regained his feet.

One leg gave him trouble, and he was only able to hobble a few paces farther before being shot in the back.

Morgan yelled in anger and frustration, too far away to actually help. And the battle was too loud, too confusing for the soldiers to pay attention even if they had heard him.

John Bowles, Chief of the Cherokee in Texas, rose up from the ground one last time. He crossed his arms and legs and waited for his death. He would not have to wait long.

The Texans held up. Afraid of a defeated old man or one of their own . A single man broke through their ranks, grabbed the Chief by his hair and put a pistol to the back of his head.

Lilian cradled her baby in one arm and placed the other on her child's shoulder.

Morgan's whole world twisted into the darkness from the year before. The same man who had killed both his father and grandfather back in Georgia was here now. And about to pull another trigger.

"Captain Hertzig, stop," one of his own troops shouted. "Don't do it!"

From his polished boots to his red silk kerchief headgear, he looked the part of the noble Indian fighter and a scurvy pirate Captain forged into one bear of a man.

In an odd way, it made sense that Captain Hertzig was at this very spot. At this very time. Georgia was too civilized for the likes of him, and Texas had busted wide open since Mexico's defeat. Ripe for a man to come and grab as much land and power as he could hold in his fists. He would have been well known for his deeds during the Trail of Tears. Perhaps even considered a hero. A top choice to join in on the crusade. Even if he wasn't asked, he would have been here. He had a taste for it.

The pistol bucked and roared. Captain Hertzig held the corpse up by his hair, taking a moment in the unnatural quiet after his pistol silenced the field.

The Captain disappeared as knife-wielding leeches swarmed in on the Chief's still twitching corpse. They carved out bloody trophies in celebration of their great victory. Hertzig re-emerged, standing in the heart of the feeding frenzy. The Cherokee sword held to the heavens in his blood-drenched fist.

"We have to leave," Morgan's mother whispered.

They had traveled North for a few hours and hadn't seen anyone since the Bowles' execution. A silence held between mother and son. Catherine had cried out once, but her mother's milk was all she needed. They were wading a slow moving stream when they heard a single musket report from somewhere behind them.

At first, Morgan thought it signaled another skirmish breaking out. He had been pulling his mother along with all the might a boy could muster until her hand pulled away.

Morgan staggered forward and, after a great deal of effort, regained his balance. The boy turned and held out his hand to her, but to no avail. Blood soaked the front of her homespun dress.

He boy saw past his mother, at the sole, red-kerchiefed horseman who was some two hundred yards downstream.

The rider paused, as if he was trying to clear a child-sized ghost from his eyes.

"I need you to take your sister," his mother said in a voice labored and strained, "and I need your gun, Morgan."

"It can't fire, Momma. I gave up all of my flints."

She caressed his cheek and used her thumb to wipe away a smudge from under his eye. "But the man on the horse doesn't know that."

Morgan did what he was told and carefully exchanged the rifle for his sister. His mother didn't see the blood on the little blanket.

"Take Catherine North, to Stand Watie." She tried to clear her throat and continued in a weak, rasping voice no longer her own. "Take her and never look back."

"I promise, Momma."

She lovingly kissed her son, leaving blood smeared on his forehead. "Go."

Morgan cleared the stream at a run and just kept running until late into the night. He ran because it was what he was supposed to do. He ran because there was nothing that he could do for his mother. And he ran because falling would do his baby sister no more harm. The same musket ball that had ripped through his mother had also taken Catherine.

It was an eagle's-flight of more than four hundred miles. For any man without supplies, alone, afoot, and hunted, an impossible task.

Morgan lovingly rebundled his baby sister's cold-frail body, took his bearings from the stars and continued his journey.

CHAPTER XII

DESIRE, DISGUST & A DILEMMA

Morgan walked out of the livery with Jack in tow. They had made Justine and the toughs scatter out the back and bolted the doors afterwards.

The street was deserted, except for a well-dressed little boy playing with a crudely whittled train. It had no paint and was missing wheels. Still the best damned toy the child could imagine.

Morgan spat out more of the livery's flavoring and used the heel of his thumb to clear out his eyes better as he made for the Ambrose.

"There's a bathhouse in the Four Bits," Jack told his new friend.

He continued towards the hotel.

"What are your plans now?"

"I am going inside."

"I'll just wait out here for you."

"No."

"Then what should I do?"

"Go to jail."

"What?" Jack could not believe what he was hearing. "The others got to cut and run while I helped you."

"You helped yourself," Morgan said, "now help yourself more."

Jack was allergic to the idea of going to a six by eight chicken coop. He wanted to laugh, yell and cuss all at once. The other's cool helped gather Jack's thoughts into a single question. "Why?"

"How long since your last?"

"Um... three days. No four," he replied, pinching his eyes shut to help his memory. "I think."

"Is there an opium den in jail?"

Jack thought that that was the damnedest fool question... even though he already understood what the other man was telling him. Jack had already decided what he would do. It was just something god-awful bitter to swallow.

"You think I'll find freedom in jail?"

"No. Break your need. Then you choose."

Jack started dragging his boots off in the direction that he least wanted to head. "If you're looking for Miss Sara, she ain't in there."

"What makes you think I am?"

"I saw who opened your window this morning."

A look passed between them.

"Where did she go?"

"I don't know, but you should ask the boy."

The stranger looked at the boy and back to Jack. The unasked question was plain.

"He's her son."

Morgan took a long look over at the boy. He was five or six-ish, with straw colored, rail straight, home-cut hair and a touch of cherub fat still hugging the edges.

"Hello. What's your name?"

The little boy looked up. "You're covered in poop."

The grownup chuckled and wiped some of the mess from his neck. "Do you know where your mother went?"

"Alexander."

"Hey Alex, how are you?"

"That way," the little conductor half-pointed.

Morgan noted the direction, thanked the boy and headed towards soap, water and somewhat clean clothes.

"I'm ok," the boy answered, "but you're still covered in poop."

Playful giggles nipped at Morgan's ankles all the way to the Ambrose. He wasn't ready for what lay in wait inside the hotel's lobby. Enos was there, affixed to his post much like the dofunnies on the walls. But it was the three daughters of the night who surprised Morgan.

"There's your vision of chivalric virtue now, ladies," Enos said, gesturing towards the Indian. Beneath the bombast, the clerk looked relieved that the "Heathen" had showed up. They would be leaving soon. Hopefully, he thought, before his wife found out that three strumpets had been lounging about his workplace.

"My name's Chloe, that's Lacy," the lady of rentable virtue said to Morgan, "and the youngster is Destiny. Señora de Anza sent us."

Chloe wasn't plump, but decidedly fat. And quite popular due to her quick tongue for subtle flattery and an everlasting seductive glance that could make a dead man's toes curl. "She wanted to thank you for what you did yesterday." The large woman looked amused at his condition, clad only in old sit-down-upons and fresh slime. It was his look of discomfort that tickled her most.

"He don't look like much, Chloe." Lacy's pock-marked face contained a rather slow look. Her public arch was the only thing that she claimed any measurable skill at. And she got paid whether a man could hang on or not. They could complain, possibly even get their next visit for free, but what man wants to admit that he wasn't enough?

The third was only known by her working name. Destiny. She was "cute," if that was the proper cut of phrase for a girl just beginning her womanly changes and still awed that she could now afford genuine store-bought dolls.

"He stinks, Chloe," Destiny handed him a token and headed out. It was brass, larger than a half dollar and stamped with one free "entertainment" redeemable only at the Four Bits.

Lacy filed by next. She put a similar token between the pressed together flesh above her corset.

Morgan smiled as he deftly removed it without actually touching her.

It was Chloe's turn. Not to be outdone, she sashayed up in front of him, tilted her head just so, pulled on his waistband and dropped the cold brass inside. Her eyes followed until it disappeared.

"Oh my God!" Chloe said. She quickly reached into her handbag and another token joined her first. "Lacy, you are so wrong. There's much to this man."

xXx

The little bell signaled Mr. Cartman he had a customer. The bell lied.

In walked the Major's men. A thicker "Rogue's Galley" one would be hard put to assemble. They were torn up, smelled worse and looked mad enough to chew on a skillet and spit nails.

Longhorn was at the forefront. "We need guns, now!"

Before the store owner could answer, they started to break things. Before he could run, they started in on him.

xXx

Clean, clothed and armed, Morgan left the Ambrose. Jack was gone when he hit the street. So was Alex. Although the boy's help was vague, Morgan knew where Sara had gone. The North end of Main street ran straight into the First Baptist Church of Calvary.

A beautiful building, well kept, well appointed and the centerpiece of the town. It had recovered from the neglect of the war years. New roof and paint. A replacement bell, for the one melted down to further the Southern Effort.

A man sat on the church's front steps. He was in his early thirties and wore a topline winter grey New Orleans-cut suit. His beaver-felt cowboy hat and gaiters were as white as mother's milk. A Colt Navy stuck out of both ends of his gunleather. Belt and holster were well worn and a fresh, thin coat of oil hugged the pistol.

Morgan slowed to exchange curt pleasantries with the man as the church doors swung full open. The Pastor smiled as he surveyed the town. Up until his gaze fell on the Cherokee.

"Where do you think you are going?"

"Inside."

"This is a house of God," the Pastor declared. "I will not allow you to taint this blessed ground."

"Your God made everything?"

"Of course."

"Then I am one of his creatures." Morgan tried again to enter but was abruptly barred.

"Yes." An old passion seeped back into the Pastor's voice. "God made the Red-man to test those of us who are his Chosen."

Morgan stood back. The clergyman was resolute. Like a gargoyle defending his threshold. The sanctuary's doors slammed shut.

The half-breed turned and started to walk away.

"I've never seen the Pastor like that. Then again I see less of him than most decent folks," the soft grey-suited man said. "Guess it's time I start though, being that I'm getting married this coming Wednesday." It was a double-dyed sense of achievement talking. Anyone near enough was bound to get an earful.

Morgan took a seat next to him.

"Wesley."

They shook hands.

"Morgan."

"Yup, I'm a lucky man. Been after her since before the War. She never did give a damn for me. Positively hated my family. Then about three months ago, she walked up to me in the middle of the street, bold as brass, and asked me if I still wanted to marry her." Wesley wasn't just telling the story, he was reliving it. "It was like a bolt out of the blue. She was crying and everything."

"Man chases woman until she catches him."

The interruption broke off Wesley's telling. He thought about what was said, and it left a warm, full smile behind.

"So what brings you to Calvary?"

"A woman."

One of the church's doors opened and Sara Mae walked out. Both men stood up. Wesley tore off his war bonnet while Morgan made to tip his.

Sara appeared frayed. Fresh sign of hours of tears and worry.

Wesley watched as she went from joy to fear as she looked from Morgan to him. The groom-to-be was going to introduce them, but his tongue was struck dead. So was his heart.

A ruckus herded towards them from down the street. It was the selfsame pack of men from the livery, less the red-headed deceiver.

It had taken some time for them to regroup. They were different this time. Fist and shovel were replaced by six-shooters and longarms. Dogbite's newfound limp forced him to bring up the rear. Not one to be caught dry a second time, he held a double-barreled fowler in each hand.

"Wes, Ms. Sara, move away from that Sumbitch," Longhorn commanded. "He's gonna pay for what he done."

Wesley was still wooly-headed in hurt. He couldn't understand why his father's crew was about to shoot a man, mid-morning, in the center of town and on the steps of the church. "What's going on?"

"That man killed your brother!" Longhorn answered. It was an excuse. Their thirst for the stranger's blood had nothing to do with Toby's death. Earlier had been about money. Now it was personal.

The Major's daughter had paid top dollar to have the breed driven from the town. Or killed, if he was too disagreeable.

This was too public for her taste. So she had cut her losses. Besides, her father's men would do him in now just to regain some of their own bravado.

"Buck's dead?" Wesley asked.

"No, Toby is," Longhorn explained, "but he also tore into Buck something fierce."

Wesley turned to his newfound friend, now enemy. "Did you kill my brother?"

"Probably."

"What does that mean?"

"I was too busy pulling triggers to make their acquaintance."

"Sara, go back inside." Wesley moved as if he was trapped in a bad dream. His pistol cleared leather.

Chapter XIII

Heartbreak, Loathing & the Devil

"No!" Sara screamed. She started towards them both, in a vain attempt to do something, anything, to stop the bloodshed.

Wesley glanced her way and Morgan took advantage.

He moved so fast that it made the evryone else look as if they had forgotten how. In a single bullwhip-like strike, Morgan slipped behind the heartsick man, captured Wesley's gun hand with his own and drew his own grapeshot pistol with the other. The Lemat speared over Wesley's left collarbone and aimed dead center of Longhorn's chest.

Still trapped, Wesley's Colt continued up and was curled inward, until the muzzle poked against the little soft spot behind where his jaw and ear met. It was angled upwards, pressed stern and forced Wesley's other ear against the half-breed's forearm, as if he was trying to spill water out of his head.

Sara stopped short. Morgan and Wes were so intertwined that she didn't know what to do.

Longhorn was leading the pack. He'd learned a long time ago that leaders were not laborers, and he hadn't exactly gotten along with hard work since he'd been weaned. In the past, he'd barked orders and men did what they were told. He had led through their fear, and this came easy to him. Now they awaited his command. If Wesley would die here, the Major would surely kill him in some unpleasant Injun-torturing way that he had learned while fighting the redskinned savages. But he knew he would never live that long as he stared up both barrels of that sumbitch's pistol.

"Shoot him." Wesley commanded.

They stood about. Not wanting to kill the Major's son by mistake. A few widened out, treating Longhorn as if the half-breed's aim could give a man the plague.

"Shoot him!" Wesley felt a subtle change come over the man who held his life by a thread. The man relaxed and his breathing slowed, as if he was more at home bringing war and death than window shopping or walking about a city. Wes tensed up, closed his eyes and wondered who would take care of Sara.

Longhorn had noticed none of this. He motioned the men to fan out farther, hoping that the pistol would track on someone, anyone, else.

The church's double doors reopened as the Pastor came out to see what the commotion on his doorstep was all about.

"Go to ground, Preacher," Longhorn spoke, relieved by the interruption.

Longhorn could not walk away, could not back down again. If he could only get that leadslinger to just track off him for an instant. Maybe, Longhorn thought, he could squeeze in a kill-shot without leaving a scratch on Wes. Just about as likely as a herd of fish stampeding though town and rescuing him. He could see no way out and no way to back down.

"Come back in about a minute because this Sumbitch is going to need you to spout out a few of them flowery church-words over his dead body."

"I'll tolerate no violence on my front steps."

Longhorn laughed. It was strained, forced to appear as if he were in control. "You got a gun, Preacher? No? Well, I guess what you'll tolerate matters less than a bucket of warm spit."

The challenge grated on the Pastor's old furnace-place of belief. To stand against the wolves is just one of the aspects of a good

Shepherd. His finger shot upwards as if to summon heavenly intervention and....

Longhorn fired. It was a risky play and he knew it. Longhorn had aimed his pistol with an exaggerated flourish, counting on the savage's professionalism not to fire back. It was a ploy to get that damned double-barrel to waver. Or maybe Sara would cry out and get him to look. Or....

But the pistol sights remained. Steady as a commandment. And death waited.

The church doors slammed shut, locked tighter than a skinflint's wallet.

"That'll be enough boys. Throw'em down." Sheriff Taylor's voice boomed out the order as if he were on a military parade ground. He had come up from the same direction as the others and was now positioned behind them, in clear view of those on the church steps.

"Aw come on, Sheriff. He's just a drifter, and you can see plain as your nose that he's attacked Wes." Longhorn pleaded their case, not wanting to be buffaloed twice in one day.

"Your choice, but I'm done asking nicely."

"No, Longhorn. Shoot him," Wes ordered, but he saw that the Sheriff had them saddled and curried.

"Please, kill him." Wes tried to struggle, but for all of it, the effort came out lame. In a small voice, filled with an inside sickness that only comes from a love that has curdled. "Please, kill me."

Again, the toughs started to drop or lay down their artillery.

"Ain't you gonna say it?" Sal looked at Longhorn.

"What?"

Sal cranked his face into an ugly imitation of the other man. "*Sumbitch.*"

Sheriff Taylor had them move away from their guns.

"Ok, mister. Now let Wesley go and throw down your guns."

The stranger let go of his bullet shield, holstered his pistol and slipped Wes' six-shooter into his own belt.

"I told you to drop 'em," Taylor said as he put his hands in his pockets. It didn't matter much where the Sheriff stuck his meat hooks because he wasn't packing iron. "And I'm done asking you."

"Why?"

"Because I told you to."

"Why?"

"They were going to kill him, J. D," Sara said.

"I can see that."

"Then why?" Morgan asked.

"For the murder of Mrs. Hertzig."

The newcomer was in the middle of setting the pistols down at his feet when he stopped cold. Still bent over, he looked into the Sheriff's eyes. The Lawman was as serious as a trainwreck. Morgan slowly disarmed, even laying out his Arkansas Toothpick and a small pocket folder that was used for everyday work.

The Sheriff picked up one of the discarded pistols and motioned for Longhorn and his crew to get moving.

"Sara. I need you to go tell Mr. Cartman that his guns are out in front of the church."

Wesley walked away, barely noticed, and ambled for nowhere; any place that wasn't here.

The town started to trickle out to watch and was lining both sides of the street as the Sheriff escorted them towards the jail. He walked beside Morgan, but trailed all of the Major's men.

"You're lucky you have the Sheriff here to protect you." Longhorn called back.

"Like at the livery?"

"Next time we'll kill you, you sumbitch," Longhorn yelled.

"Like at the livery?"

They walked on, Longhorn, Sal and the rest, throwing a fuss every step of the way.

With safety assured, the townsfolk poured out in droves. Women pulled their children to their breast, shielding them from the sight, while they watched spell-bound. Men speculated among themselves as to what was happening.

"Bless you, Sheriff for saving us," came from the rear of the crowd. They seemed more relieved that the half-breed stranger was off their streets than anything else.

J. D. ignored it all, not allowing his attention to slip a hair's breadth. He got them off the street and into his office without any further trouble.

Jack was the only current resident of the jailhouse's two cells. Tucked up under a blanket and dead to the world.

Sheriff Taylor stuck the Major's men into the empty one and the stranger in with Jack.

"Time to go, Jack," J. D. told the lump of blankets. It took a doing, but Jack got up and shuffled out.

"Sheriff?" the stranger asked. "Can you give Jack my money and make sure he gets a bed at the Ambrose?"

"I'll do that, only if you promise not to try anything in my jail."

"You have nothing to fear from me."

The Sheriff thought about the answer. "That's good enough for me."

The two cells faced each other across the center walkway, with no backdoor. Longhorn called out as the Sheriff began to shut a reenforced door that cut off the cells from his office.

"Hey, Sheriff."

J. D. didn't bother a glance as he put the key in the lock.

"This ain't done with yet!"

"I don't know what exactly happened at Isaiah's," he shut the cell door and cranked the key, "but I bet you said something similar at the livery."

xXx

The Pastor slumped and let his forehead come to rest on the doors. He could swear that the bullet had hit him, imagined it spearing through his ribs. His body felt as if it had become somehow wooden.

Hiram turned and started walking slowly up the aisle, checking to see if he had gotten creased. He discovered what he was looking for. The bullet had missed him, but it had punched a hole in his jacket. He quickly felt and found a second hole. The lead had drilled out the jacket's back also. Unbelieving, Hiram removed the coat to stare at the damage. He draped it on the pulpit and looked up from the coat to the wooden figure nailed upon the cross.

It had been a long time since he had looked, really looked, up to the Savior, although he had been there all along.

That is when Hiram noticed it. Longhorn's bullet had continued its path and struck the sculpture's side.

Sometimes a simple event can shatter a decayed or decadent person. Especially if the soul was already aware of the sin.

Hiram fell to his knees in pieces, helpless before the freshly wounded son of the King of Kings.

And he prayed.

xXx

The news galloped its way to the Major's ear before his men were within sight of the hoosegow. Being the richest, most powerful, admired and feared man in three or more counties had its advantages.

The whole town was afraid to step out and take a piss.

As the last rays of sunlight gave up and retreated against the darkness, he arrived, wearing storeboughts and driving a leather lined carriage. Looking all the part of respectable town elder.

They'd expected his blood-trimmed uniform, mounted on his magnificent grey Appaloosa with Hell following.

But he had only brought his Justine.

His daughter sat silently, dressed as the perfect and prim lady in mourning. The only thing she lacked was an expression. It wasn't of dried tears or the rigid pose of the grief stricken. To onlookers, the Major's daughter seemed to have fully recovered from her mother's passing in a remarkably quick fashion.

The Major greeted those who came out with well practiced affection. He made small talk about their children or inquired how prosperous their business was or about the coming storm.

After seeing that it was safe, Kingston Pitt, Calvary's Mayor, came out and suckled up to the Hertzigs the rest of the way. They spoke shortly, and the Mayor agreed with every "request" that Mr. Hertzig made.

The town became a bustle of activity in the Major's wake, intent to catch up on the labors that they had left off as they waited.

The buggy came to a halt at the Sheriff's Office just as J. D. came out to meet them.

The Major got down, groaning wryly as he worked the kinks out of his back.

"Sheriff."

"Major. Justine. Mr. Pitt."

"Heard you picked up some scraggly redback for killing Mrs. Hertzig." The Major went on with only a token wait for the Sheriff's reply. "I want to see him."

Taylor stepped to one side and held the door open as if it was his duty.

"Stay," the Major commanded his daughter.

The Mayor made to tag along but was cut short by a glare. "I'll just stay out here and keep your lovely daughter company...." It was almost put as a question, as Mr. Pitt kicked a few pebbles under the jail's boardwalk.

The Major turned away and continued on in. The office known for its stale coffee and a warm smile had been transformed into an armory. There were stacks of rifles and shotguns placed strategically about. All different makes and models of pistols were in evidence too. Most of those were supplied by a circuit judge's gavel. Full boxes of bullets had been ripped opened to ease reloading. Loose powder, percussion caps and lead balls were in neat piles on the Sheriff's desk.

Sheriff Taylor's gun leather was heaped in his chair, as if it had just been put there as he ran to hold open the door.

"Were you expecting someone?" The Major surveyed the arsenal, knowing full well that the Sheriff had forted up. Some would call the Sheriff prudent, but the Major enjoyed the panic he still commanded.

The words only made J. D. more uncomfortable. He felt that he had just insulted the Major. Recent events left him no choice, he told himself. Part and parcel of the job. Leastways his town was safe, and that was all that really mattered.

Major Hertzig was past him and into the back before the Sheriff had a chance to fish the keys out from the lock.

As he entered, his crew stood up, cheering, and hooting. It had only been a few hours, but they all had had enough of being penned up.

The Major continued down the aisle and came to a halt in front of the stranger. Fists poised on his hips, and on his face was an air of self-righteous superiority.

The stranger sat at the end of the bunk, head down and fixed in place. His long black hair hung loosely, making it impossible for the Major to get a good look at his face.

"What is this? Some kind of joke?" The Major cast about, looking for someone who looked the part of a man who could take down six good men single-handed. Someone bigger. Someone meaner. Someone a damn sight tougher.

"No joke, Major."

"You're telling me that that... this ragamuffin-breed is the cause of all of this commotion?"

Sheriff Taylor held up his hands, palms upwards, signaling that he could not add anything more to what he had already said.

"Hell, Sheriff, I've scraped better men off my shoe."

The Major swivelled his attention back to the prisoner.

"Heard what you did in the livery." It was more a command than a statement. "I've earmarked you as pure trouble."

But the object of his scorn sat unmoved.

"I'd kill you myself for putting your filthy hands on my Justine, but I've decided that I'll let the law handle you."

"Kills-In-Water was one."

"What?"

"Oliver Robert Black was two."

Major Hertzig and the Sheriff exchanged baffled glances.

"Lilian-"

"That's enough," the Indian fighter decreed in a voice that was too loud and abrupt. "I don't know what this is about, or if you're just some damned fool that spews out babble, but that's enough."

"Black," the warrior went on as if the Major had said nothing at all. "daughter of Kills-In-Water of the Wolf clan, was three."

The Major had heard this kind of bellyaching all before, and often enough to set a pocket watch by it. A well seasoned fire-eater doesn't get three steps without hearing that kind of shit from every braggart and two-bit bravo that ever crossed his shadow. The lowest kind were the crybabies with a tear-jerking story, accusing him of a passel of crimes and demanding justice.

None had dared for several years now. For he was respectable now. Powerful beyond most measuring sticks. The Major interrupted again, "Listen close, boy. I don't know any of those names. I don't have a clue as to who you are. So you think I wronged you and now I should give a damn?" the Major laughed.

"Normally a murderer like yourself would have to wait for the Circuit Judge to roll on through here, but I've taken the liberty of speaking to the Mayor about you. And he's agreed that it'd be best to have this affair settled quickly."

J. D. patted Major Hertzig on the shoulder in a gesture that said it was time to leave.

"You know what that means, boy?" the Major went on, not expecting an answer. "It means in a few short days, I'll have the pleasure of watching you *waltz* at the end of a rope."

"Time to go, Major."

"Ok, Sheriff, but will you make sure your prisoner has enough hankies." The Major was all smiles as he slapped J. D. on the back. "Now let's you and me have a chat about you setting my boys free so I can get about my business."

They turned and made it to the doorway.

"For what you have done, I will kill you."

The words themselves didn't bother the Major, but it was how they were said that ripped into him like a head wound. Plain as water. And with about the same emotion one puts into telling a stranger the time of day. It wasn't said loud, but it burrowed deep. Behind bars and about to get a onetime invite to a necktie social, yet they were said with such conviction as if it had already happened.

"And this time," the prisoner continued, "I will not hesitate."

"You're a sumbitch," Longhorn said as he tried to regain a slice of his manhood, "that's what you are!"

Morgan stood and walked to the bars. As he came forward, Longhorn and his crew retreated a step or two. Even with two sets of bars between them, he'd earned a healthy respect.

There was something in his hands. Something small. That no one had noticed until now, or hadn't bothered to look. He flipped it at the Major, who caught it through sheer reflex.

"This is yours."

CHAPTER XIV

A BOY'S INNOCENCE, A FATHER'S SIN

"You ok, Mommy?" Alex asked.

Sara pulled her face from her hands to see her son at the bottom of the church steps, looking too worried for one so young. She was choked up and called for a hug with her hands.

Her boy smiled. It was an open-mouthed, teeth showing, "oh-boy, I getta hug from my mommy" smile that would warm a mother's soul and melt away heartache quicker than any medicine.

He flew up the steps and into his mother's arms. And it was just what Sara needed.

"Why are you sitting out here, Mommy?"

"Alexander, Mommy has to make a hard decision. Either choice will hurt somebody." Without breaking the embrace, she smooched his cheek. "And Mommy doesn't know what to do."

"That's silly, Mommy. You always know the right thing to do."

Sara was startled. The *right* thing. Maybe she was reading too much into what her son had said, but sometimes a five year old can lay plain a problem that adults heap all sorts of complexities on. Yes, Sara knew that she'd done wrong with the stranger. But she could never let a man hang for a crime that he didn't do. She would be shamed from the town once the townsfolk knew, that was for certain. Or run out.

Plus there was the marriage to Wesley that she could no longer go through with anyway.

She would tell the Sheriff, but only after she had completed preparations to leave first for Alexander's sake.

Besides, she thought as a smile played across her lips, maybe the stranger would want to come with them. But that was pure hope and dreams, Sara knew that he wasn't the marrying-type. Besides, few men were willing to step into a fatherhood already started five and a half years earlier.

Sara turned her son until he was sitting on her lap, leaving the hug in place. "Alex, Sweetpea, Mommy needs to talk to you...."

xXx

Major Hertzig looked down at what lay in his hand. It was made from leather and appeared to be a small pouch, about the size used for plug cut tobacco fixings. The drawstring was braided from long red hair, not unlike the color of his daughter's.

The Major laughed again. But this time it was a mocking, contempt-filled, burst. He checked the pouch's weight and rubbed it between his fingers, trying to determine what secrets it held inside.

"You stupid heathen." The Major's disgust was at full bore. "There is nothing inside this little bag that can spook me. No totem. No Medicine Man's magic. Nothing."

His men laughed and hooted. No one bested the Major. Ever. And to see their enemy as just a dumb savage took the sting from their own failures.

The Major loosened the drawstring and gazed into it. A look of amusement on his face.

An illness overtook the Major, swift as a hurled lightning bolt. So unexpected that the pouch fell from his numb fingers. He grimaced in pain and clutched at his chest.

There was a shocked silence, only disturbed by J. D.'s frantic efforts to shore up the Major and help him retreat to the front office.

Longhorn, Dogbite, Sal and the rest heard the Major choke up his grub before the Sheriff came back in, picked up the discarded pouch and left, slamming the door shut on the way out. There was a newfound look about them, one of confusion and fear, not that any of them would admit it, but it was unmistakable as a sunset on the prairie.

Longhorn looked down at the spot where the bag had been, then up at the half-breed who was yanking out long strands of hair from the back of his head. Longhorn knew that he'd never understand the peculiar ways of the Redman. It didn't matter though, because all the grieving in the world wouldn't save the sumbitch now.

"You jes dug your own grave."

xXx

Enos was sweeping off the boardwalk when Alex whisked by him and inside the Ambrose. Sara's young'un wasn't as intolerable as most, but that'd change in time, Enos knew. They all changed in time.

The clerk stopped sweeping. Maybe the little scamp was already up to something. Enos hurried after him.

"Stop right there, boy!"

Alex froze. On his tippytoes and standing on top of the hotel's desk, with his fingers barely reaching the musician's sword that hung from the wall.

"What do you think you're doing?"

The little boy pulled the sword free, regained his balance and turned to face the grownup.

"I am now Sir Alexander," he proclaimed as he raised the sword as if he were a knight facing a vile dragon.

"That was your father's. Put it back where it belongs."

Alex started forward, pouty-faced, holding the sword up high.

The old clerk wasn't to be done in by a five year old, so he stood there, barring the way.

"Mr. Naggy, my father ran away and hurt Mom. Now he's dead. He don't need it anymore."

"Put it back this very instant!" Enos said. He shifted his hold on the broom, copying the boy. He held for a moment, but when the boy advanced he gave ground, until Alex was past him and crossing the street.

"I'll tell your mother!"

The little rascal threw the livery door wide and the sounds of Isaiah's steady hammerwork seemed to rise up from within. Alex marched in, sword held high in triumph.

The last thing Enos saw before the door closed was Alexander's face, scrunched up from the effort of sticking his tongue out as far as he possibly could.

xXx

The Major held on to the desk as if it was a piece of a shipwreck and the only thing keeping him from slipping beneath the pitch-black waves. He waited until he'd mostly recovered.

"Sheriff."

"Major?"

"What are the charges?"

"Assault. Theft. Disturbing the Peace." Taylor left out the attempted murder his men tried on the church steps. It wouldn't stick and would only serve to stir up the Major even more. Besides, if this whole nasty business didn't go away in two shakes of a lamb's tail it'd hurt his town something fierce.

"I'm here to get my boys."

"You know that I can't do that, Major," J. D. said in a sympathetic manner, "plus there's still the matter of what they did to Mr. Cartman. Roughed him up pretty good and stole a bunch of guns."

"We both know that little Jew has no intention of filing charges."

They were bitter words for J. D. to hear. The Major was telling the truth, but that didn't make it right. Mr. Cartman was a good man. A hard worker. Never anything but kindness. He had a courage about him. A quiet kind that wasn't strapped to his leg, or found at other people's expense. They had treated him poorly for years and gotten away with it. J. D. had no expectations that this time would be any different. Hell, the Major had probably already sent someone to make sure Mr. Cartman would remain quiet as ever.

The Major pulled out his billfold and laid out more money than J. D. had ever seen outside the bank. It barely dented the Major's pocket money.

"There. A hundred dollars a head should cover the guns they bought." He used a spare red kerchief to wipe away the sickness that didn't make it to the floor. When he looked up into the Sheriff's eyes, the old Major started to return with a vengeance.

"Now, you let my boys go."

xXx

It had been hours since J. D. had let the Major's men go, but it still wasn't sitting well with him. The front door opened slowly, giving him time to stop scribbling away at his daily log and ready a handgun.

It was Alex, Sara's little boy, who peeked his head in, and it nearly took a few years off the Sheriff's life. He uncocked the pistol and returned it to the drawer.

"Come on in, son. What's on your mind?"

"My Mommy wants me to give this to Mr. Black," Alex said as he held up their family Bible. His mother had to clean off the dust before she had given it to him. It hadn't been opened since she woke up to an empty bed.

J. D. smiled. "Well, come here and let me have a look."

He had always thought that religion never hurt nobody, especially behind bars. Normally, he'd have just let the boy in with the book. But "normal" had left with the arrival of the last stage.

The boy placed it in the man's outstretched hand and J. D. flipped through it before handing it back. No gun. No key or file, but a single folded paper floated free and to the floorboards.

The Sheriff raised an eyebrow towards Alex and scooped it up.

"You know anything about this?"

"No, Sir."

Sheriff Taylor could see the truth for what it was. The little boy was innocent. And that only left Sara.

"I'll give *Mr. Black* the Bible."

"But Mom told me to do it."

"You just did, son. You gave it to me, and I'll give it to him. That's how things work in a jail. Now, run along and promise me that you'll give your mom my best?"

"Yes, Sir." Alex saluted and made for the door. "Sheriff Taylor?"

"What is it, son?"

"You know he didn't hurt Mrs. Hertzig and you should let him go, right?"

"How would you know this?"

"My mommy told me," Alex said with a smile too big for his little face. He shut the door as he left. The boy had brought more questions than answers.

J. D. rocked back in his buffalo hide chair, the Bible in one hand and the no longer hidden note in the other. Things just couldn't get any stranger, he thought as he opened the letter. He couldn't have been more wrong if he had worked at it.

"I'll be damned."

xXx

It was breakfast time before Morgan had any other company. Both Jack and the Sheriff carried in a cloth covered plate. Wisps of steam curled up, bringing with it a hint of the Ambrose's finest.

Jack stood aside and J. D. was the first to speak.

"You didn't kill her, did you?"

"No," Morgan answered, "but what makes you ask now?"

"This," the Sheriff said as he put the letter atop the food. "Seems your whereabouts are spoken for...."

Jack pulled off the linen, stuck it in his shirtfront and started to eat.

"I have room now, so I thought it best to dry out Jack a bit more."

"I am free then?" Morgan asked.

"Well that's... complicated."

The prisoner gave him a look that said he needed an explanation.

"You see, the whole town thinks you're a woman-killer." Taylor rubbed the back of his neck, buying a moment to collect his words.

"And if you'd walk about before I clear this thing up, you'll be shot on sight."

The Sheriff handed the plate to Jack and unlocked Morgan's cell. "I'll bring a game of checkers to help pass the time."

Jack went in and gave his friend the other plate, letter and all.

J. D. had never been close to any woman. He had chosen long ago to be married to the badge. There weren't that many good women about and those deserved better than a "son-of-a-whore" Sheriff. But he understood that there was something already unmistakable between Sara and this man. Saw it in her face, plain as the written word, when he went and talked to her about the letter.

"She needs the time," J. D. told his prisoner.

Morgan's face told the Sheriff what he needed to know.

"Hey," Jack exclaimed to Morgan, "you got two pieces of pie and I didn't get a one!"

xXx

Sheriff Taylor rode over the same cobblestones that he'd traveled two nights ago. Everything was different now. He was alone, except for his horse. The morning was thick with fog. It seemed as if his entire world had been recast in various shades of grey overnight. The cloud cover was a darker blend of the same, holding a cutting chill between the pecan trees.

J. D. knew that he was drawing close when he spied the cannon, lit only by the unsteady lamplight that escaped from the mansion.

After the second knock, the door swung open to reveal Buck. He was battered, bandaged and about as pleased as a one legged dog without a tree. Buck motioned for the Sheriff to come inside.

He removed his hat upon entering, not sure if it was what he should do in such a house, but the interior was awe-inspiring. J. D. regretted that he hadn't taken a bath first.

Major Johannes Hertzig appeared on the second floor landing and started to descend the main staircase. He was dressed for bed, except for the red kerchief about his head.

"Do you like the vestibule?"

The Sheriff quickly glanced about, trying to figure out which piece of the furnishings was a "vestibule."

The Major chuckled, "The entrance hall, I mean the room you're standing in."

J. D. could plainly see that the Major had recovered from earlier that day. Maybe over-recovered....

"It's good you came." Hertzig was all smiles as they shook hands. "Shall we move to the library?"

The Sheriff had never seen a library before. This was no room just to read a book in. It was a gentleman's domain, an inner sanctum where the Major could be at peace and shut out the rest of the world. The room was done all in dark, manly colors and was filled with paintings.

The built-in bookshelves ran from the polished oak floor to the vaulted ceiling that had rococo plaster work and roundels depicting biblical stories carved into them. The shelves held more than books also. There were fine-crafted wooden boxes and a bust of a frumpy-looking Roman emperor.

In one corner, a Confederate uniform hung on a wooden dummy. It was pretty as a picture and only came out for Sunday service and special occasions. The uniform was complete, less the regulation headgear.

Centered and to the rear of the chamber was a desk that put the Sheriff's to shame, both in size and grandeur. It had a single mammoth, leather-bound book atop it and a matching throne-like chair. To either side was a pair of chest-high globes, one of the earth and the other of the heavens.

"Something to drink? A cigar?" the Major asked in a pleasant voice.

"I'm not staying long, Major."

"I know. How 'bout a jar of that fine pomegranate jam to take with you?" Johannes stuck his head out the door and yelled up instructions to his daughter.

J. D. resigned himself. He was uncomfortable and meandered about, still taking in the room. "I'm here on business."

"I know."

"You know?"

The Major chuckled, "Of course, our good Mayor has already asked me to be the judge at the Indian's trial." The Major held out his hand to receive the papers making it official.

"The Indian is no longer suspected of killing your wife."

"What?"

J. D. could see that the Major started to look ill again. He repeated himself, slower this time, and stuck an apology on its tail.

"Now why is that, Sheriff?" he said in a lowered tone.

"I have a witness. Knows where he was all night."

"All night?" the Major asked, looking rather skeptical.

"Yes, sir."

"And this person is... believable?"

"Absolutely."

"You haven't thought this out, have you?" The Major joined J. D. in front of the uniform.

"I understand that you're disappointed, Major, but the fact is the stranger's whereabouts have been spoken for," J. D. said, "and I need you to call off your boys."

"I can't do that."

"Why not? You now know he didn't kill your wife."

The Major shook his head. "It's not about that. It's about what comes next."

Justine tapped on the door as she entered, wearing a bearskin overcoat mostly covering an ankle-length nightgown. Her rose-red lips held a bewitching smile. She had brought the jam.

J. D. blushed and turned his attention back to the Major's question.

"Next?" The Sheriff was baffled. He could nearly always tell which way a conversation was headed, but this time he had lost the scent.

"What are you planning to do after you release him?" The Major turned away from J. D. and busied himself by preening the uniform.

A simple question. One that had to be answered careful-like. When Sheriff Taylor had learned that Morgan had nothing to do with Mrs. Hertzig's death, he suspected that more was afoot than he reckoned with. It could have been one the Major's men who had killed Mrs.

Hertzig. Or maybe even something far more sinister. Either way, there was a pure danger involved. He also figured that before the Major would fall on his own sword, he would give up the murderer. Hell, the Major'd probably kill one of his men and pin something incriminating on the body, just to tie up the loose ends, pretty as a church social.

"Don't you worry, Major, I'll find out who killed your wife."

"Daddy?"

The Major drew the saber from the uniform's sword belt, spun around and, in one fluid lunge, thrust it through J. D.'s heart.

A saber is made to slice. Flexible. To take advantage of a mount's weight and speed. Not for the thrust of a straight blade. With a quarter twist, he had guided the blade between the Sheriff's ribs. The distance from sword point to flesh was closed in one direct, snake-strike. The footwork, the straightening sword arm, and all the rest combined with such harmony as to leave four inches of steel sticking out the Sheriff's back.

"I believe you," the Major said as the Sheriff's legs buckled and his body slid off the saber.

CHAPTER XV

SECRETS

"You didn't have to do that," Justine stated.

The Major walked up to his daughter, delicately touched her cheek and ran his thumb roughly over her lips. She closed her eyes and gasped slightly. They opened to the sight of his thumb smeared in rose-red.

"When you came downstairs, all painted up for bed and wearing my coat, I had no other choice."

Justine glanced down at the warm bearskin and smiled coyly. The nightgown could be explained, but her father was right about the rest. The bedrock of his empire would have cracked. With the Sheriff's blood still seeping, her thoughts were already calculating how best to turn this to her advantage. "But he had no idea that I killed her."

"Nope, and he probably would've never found out," her father said, wiping the saber clean on the dead man's wool shirt.

"So why did you kill him?" She knew why, but would never directly confront him. He would never stand for it. So she'd play her part, until an opportunity arose. Like that of a dead Sheriff in her father's library. Justine smiled.

"A man like the Sheriff is kinda like a dog. He would've dug about 'til he uncovered... other *secrets* along the way." Johannes inspected the blade, to whitewash his discomfort over such a dishonorable topic of conversation.

"You have become so brazen," he whispered.

"It was you who hired Mr. Franks to kill mother. You wanted her dead." Justine's words were meant to rake him, but more important, to throw any blame off of her.

"You know nothing."

"You *needed* her dead."

"Yes, but not like this."

"Well your way cost you a son," she said. Her whole manner became taunting. "And your hired killer was a complete failure."

"No!" His hand cutt off her next comment as he raised his voice. "Any idiot could have killed her. He had no idea what he was being hired to do."

"Then what was he hired for, Daddy?"

"Mr. Franks was here to take the blame."

"I... don't understand?" All her attitude drained away.

Her father sighed. The Major had hoped Justine would have figured it out on her own. He needed her to be more cunning.

Tobias, his youngest son, was loyal as a puppy, good at being told what to do. But that wasn't what the Major needed for his legacy to live on. Plus, Toby had disqualified himself by getting killed.

There was Buck. He was as dull as a cannonball and half as sharp. That would never do.

Wesley? Annoyingly good hearted. Honorable. Yet such the momma's boy. He was smart, maybe too smart for his own good, but he had no *vision*. No understanding of the importance of breeding.

That left only his daughter. Or did it? If she were only to give him a....

He went on, "The stagecoach is robbed and everyone is killed. All but one, a remorseless killer-for-hire." He pinched his trigger finger and thumb together at each point, as if he were killing lice. "He rides back to San Antonio on one of the team's horses. And when the Sheriff gets around to searching him they would have found two thousand dollars. The same amount my bank placed on the stage for me. He'd have swung, or, better still, died trying to shoot his way clear."

"Couldn't he have buried it outside town and picked it up after all this had blown over?"

"Sure, he could," her father continued, "but not Mr. Franks. He'd have been too busy steaming that I didn't hire him to think about being set-up. And too arrogant to hide the money."

"How could you be so certain?"

"You can always count on sin."

"How was this all supposed to work out, I mean... the money and all?"

"They worked for me. Quinn led them. Good boys too, well salted to that kind of work." He sat down behind his desk and started to test the sword's sharpness with his fingertips. "Once it was done, Quinn was to hand two thousand dollars, of my money, to Mr. Franks and tell him that his services were no longer needed."

"But why go to all the trouble?" Justine asked.

"That's a good question." He was somewhat relieved, his daughter was learning quickly. "If the passengers are killed during a robbery, that's understandable. If half a dozen passengers are just killed, people will want to know why. Either way, people want to hold someone accountable."

"And that's what Mr. Franks was for."

"Now, be a good girl and tell Buck to round up the boys," her father told her, but she didn't move.

"So what do we do now?"

"I will introduce the Sheriff to the bottom of the lake." He went on before her surprise was voiced into a question. "And I tell the towners the truth... that it's a mystery to where the Sheriff left off to, but that we must replace him becuase, for the good of Calvary, we must move forward."

"But Daddy, won't people wonder or even suspect?"

"Some, but that can work for me too." He laid the sword atop the mammoth book. The Hertzig family tree. The history of all that was Hertzig. His legacy.

Justine knew that her father was deadly and could twist any

situation to his favor, but none of that was what she needed to know.

"So what about me?"

The question took roost between them. Unanswered. Squirming in Justine's belly.

The door was thumped at and the doorknob was bungled with until it opened, killing what was transpiring between the two....

Buck stood there, trying to look serious amid the bandages. "Widers cum."

Riders? Justine had no idea who they were. Or what business they would have at the Circle Nine. She looked to her father for answers.

"That'd be the Donathans." The Major shot them a smile. "It's time for me to stop being nice."

xXx

Jack heard someone in the front office, got up and went to the bars. He wondered what had taken the Sheriff so long. The weather was not bad enough to play a part. He didn't have long to wait. The reinforced door unlocked, but it was one of the Major's men, not Sheriff Taylor who entered. Jack knew Sal. Knew his sharp tongue and the swiftness of his yellow handled razor.

A mostly dry Sal leered at them and walked between the two cells. He brought the reek of beer with him.

And sweat.

And sex.

The winds and rain picked up, coming in uninvited through the small, barred windows.

Sal carried an old grain sack with too much care for it to be a casual thing. The smallish man kicked a game of checkers from underfoot.

"I was going to be the one to stick the noose about your neck," he bosted to the Indian, "but now that's been taken away from me."

Sal glanced at Jack, making sure that he held no threat.

"I wanted to watch as you slowly choked on your own tongue. Bet you would've looked like a turnip when you were through."

"You'll never get away with this." Jack didn't exactly know what "this" he was talking about, but he knew "this" was going to be bad.

"For what you done, I will kill you." Sal said. It wasn't a half-bad impersonation of Morgan. He laughed at his own wit and shook the sack, getting a chorus from the angry rattlesnakes held within. "But first, I'm going to sweat you, like you done us twice."

Jack looked to his newfound partner. He didn't believe that Morgan was actually asleep, but he couldn't see where lying out on the bunk was going to help either.

"The Major said that you Cherokees have a song that you sing. One that stops rattlesnakes from killing. Dogbite bet me five whole dollars that it ain't true."

"Morgan?" Jack called, but there was no reply. He continued with Sal. "The Sheriff-"

"Is dead. I helped sink the body," Sal interrupted, "and the Major's having a town meeting right now in the church, to ponder the Sheriff's disappearence and to mourn his own dearly departed wife." The last piece was said stuffed full of sarcasm. "They'll replace the Sheriff with whoever-the-hell the Major tells them to."

Sal turned his attention fully on the stranger. "You know what I got in this here bag? Rattlers. There's not much for a snake to do when it's being flung through the air, except get mad, fangs bared and ready to kill." He shook the grain sack to get another bunch of rattling, truly enjoying what he was about to do. It reminded him of getting worked up before taking a girl.

"So, I got a question for you. You going to sing? Or beg?"

"Hey, Sal?" Jack called from behind.

"What?" Sal was working the sack knot that Dogbite had tied with a half dozen too many knots. Sal was actually squeamish about handling snakes, but not about torturing others with them.

"Thanks for kicking the checker game."

Sal ignored the remark.

"I was losing."

Sal wondered what the hell that mattered? A child's game in the middle of the floor... the *middle*? He heard the low whine of a cell door as it swung open behind him. The same door that made the same protest when he was released the day before. He hurtled himself away, spinning to face Jack and succeeded in only hastening his death.

Sal had leapt too near the stranger's cell, and a thinly braided garrote, one made from long black Cherokee hair, bit deep into his neck.

Sal dropped the sack and fumbled for a weapon, but Morgan had neatly shifted both ends of the garrote into one hand and trapped Sal's wrist with the other. The razor fell from Sal's useless fingers and clattered on the hardwood floor. The only thing left for him to do was to quit breathing and die.

Sal's face swelled, turning from an angry red to a ghastly purple. His eyes bulged. An ugly gurgling escaped, but the garrote held. Panic took his bladder as Hell reclaimed his soul.

And they were not alone.

Alexander stood in the doorway that separated the office from the back. He was rain-soaked, frantic and hurt. His face was scraped, and one of his eyes hid behind the swelling. They were shocked as the little boy ran forward. Jack scooped him up before he grabbed for the straight edge.

Alex struggled, not willing to accept being caught so. What a five year old doesn't possess in strength or skills can somewhat be aided by the sharpness of revenge. That, and a well honed razor.

But they were more concerned with the boy's innocence. So Jack held on. And tried to comfort him. And Jack worried.

Morgan tied Sal's carcass up by its neck to one of the iron crossbars and went around to help.

Jack handed Alex to Morgan, and the boy cut loose with the tears. They all moved to the front office. All except the snakes.

"I'm sorry," Alexander said as broke into tears, "I didn't know what to do. I ran here as fast as I could."

"Just tell us what happened and everything'll be alright." Jack failed to calm the boy, but he could taste the sorrow even before he understood the story. An unreasonable guilt. The same pain that tore him apart and tossed the pieces into the bottle and pipe.

"No. No, it won't be. Isaiah's dead and they're hurting Mommy."

Morgan's voice was distilled of all emotion, "Where is she?"

Jack knew war. Tactics demanded a good understanding of the enemy, especially if you're outnumbered. But it'd be a waste of breath trying to talk sense into his friend right then. They were about to start a war without so much as an invite.

Morgan sat Alex down in the Sheriff's chair and told the boy to stay. The two men looked at each other and they nodded as one. They broke into action, Morgan rifled the desk as Jack went about the room, both searching for weapons or the keys to those chained to the walls.

Jack found nothing, so he ran back and looted Sal. Under the dead man's vest was a Colt Model 1849, .31 caliber, five shot. It had a four inch octagonal barrel and the standard factory scroll worked cylinder. He checked it, four loads. It was nothing special, but it would do. The straight razor lay in a puddle of piss, but Jack wasn't too proud. He picked it up and wiped it dry on the dead man's shirt.

Jack returned, showing the Colt and the knife. His friend held up a derringer.

Morgan switched out the stingy pistol for the Colt.

"Careful," Morgan said as he checked the other pistol. "It has only one shot."

Jack went over to the chained rifles and shotguns, his intent clear.

"We can't shoot the lock, it'll put them on guard. Besides, the Sheriff must have all the ammunition locked up in his safe."

"Morgan, we only have five shots between us."

Jack felt scolded when he saw Morgan's eyes. Sara was helpless and he was fretting over a bullet count. Damn, Jack thought, but if this man wouldn't kick in the gates of Hell and tie the Devil's tail to a hitching post just to teach him a some manners.

"Sal was wrong, you know. It's more like a radish than a turnip."

But his friend, with the Colt in hand, was already out the door.

CHAPTER XVI

VIOLATED & A SHOWDOWN

Sara would never forget their names. Buckley. Longhorn. Dogbite. Hoyt. Bugeye and Critter. But Sal would pay the most of all if she lived to have her way. He was the one who had lured her into Isaiah's livery. No, she would never forget them. Or forgive.

Sal had told her that her son had been hurt and needed her, that Doc Geraint had already been sent for. She ran into the trap without another thought.

They had been drinking. And although they actually had her son, they didn't want money. This was more about power and their need to spread fear, than about her flesh.

She would have screamed, but she was afraid that might cause them to hurt Alex. Sara pleaded with them to let her boy go, that she would do whatever it took just to save her son.

Alex lashed out, kicking and flailing, trying to protect his mommy as Buck half carried the boy into the tack room.

There was more scuffling until Sara heard a vulgar thud. It was too quiet when Buck returned alone.

With her son out of the way, Sara didn't wait to be a victim. Her fear and anger transformed her into a hellion. A mountain lioness fighting for both her and her cub's life. She broke Bugeye's glasses and gouged another's face. Sara punched and kicked, bit and gouged, with more might than she ever knew she possessed.

But they were too many and she could not prevail.

And turns were taken at rendering unpardonable sins....

And it went on.

And on.

Finally, it was decided. They would head back to the Circle Nine, leaving Sal to take care of the jail and Buck to clean up the livery.

Buck cinched on his thumbstall while he waited for them to file out. He knew what to do. Even a five year-old could fit a noose around a man's gizzard. Especially when it came to defiling a lady.

He hadn't taken a turn yet, content to just watch or call out instructions. Buck felt uneasy dropping his pants in front of others, but now it was just him. And a shattered, helpless woman was his for the taking. The one who had allowed an Injun to stay in her hotel. The one who had turned his disgrace into a wall trophy for all to see. Buck would've liked to have gone to the jail and watched the Injun die, or even helped Sal. But Sara had to pay and that wouldn't wait.

By taking her, he succeeded in taking what his brother Wesley had only dreamed of owning. It would restore him as a man to be feared throughout the county. And he had something to prove to his father.

Buck pulled out his Bowie knife and held it near so she could see the naked steel. For all Sara had been through, now she looked truly scared. Her fear excited him. And he descended....

It wasn't long before she started to laugh. It was a small thing at first. Through the sobbing and gasping, through the panic and pain, through the defilement and humiliation, she laughed. It built on itself as he allowed her enough air to struggle. But the laughter came out twisted. Eerie.

For his part, Buck was taken aback. He tried to slap the terror back into her eyes.

"What's so damned funny?"

"You remind me of my husband," she said as she stabbed him with his own forgotten Bowie.

He froze, with an odd, confused look on his face.

She stabbed again. And again. Sara's laugh became a manic's scream.

Buck wrapped both hands about her neck. Fear rode him hard as he squeezed. He tried to snap her neck-bone before she could hurt him anymore.

And she stabbed.

xXx

Morgan and Jack raced to the livery with Alexander pulling hard to catch up. They barreled through the doorway, and even though the boy had told them what had happened, they were struck by what they saw.

Sara lay broken. Limp. Motionless. Her pale skin had a blue tint and was drenched in blood. She was covered in scrapes and cuts, muck and bits of her own clothing. Her neck, twisted to an odd angle and altogether bruised, had taken the brunt of it.

Buck had survived the knifing long enough to drag himself away. The blood trail was a foot wide and led only a few yards to where he sat upright against a support post. His eyes seemed to refocus as Morgan entered. A chuckle leaked out. It wasn't smart, but he was far beyond caring.

Morgan recovered and handed the Colt off as he turned to clutch Alex to his chest. He squeezed the boy, shielding him from the sight. Both comforting each other's pain as a gun-shot rang out, then another, followed by an odd flat-sounding "pop" from within the livery.

xXx

Up at the North end of Calvary, the church brimmed with townsfolk and concern.

Mayor Pitt called for the meeting. Sheriff Taylor's disappearance was the issue. That, and the question of who they could get to fill in until a proper election was held.

"Now, in our hour of need, to safeguard over our beloved township and to oversee that justice is done to the filthy murderer still held within our fine jail, I propose that Mr. Franks be elected as our new Sheriff," Pitt concluded.

"You mean until we find out what really happened to Sheriff Taylor?" came from the back pews. The townsfolk were good people. Unaccustomed to such upheaval in their lives. And even less inclined towards the likes of Mr. Franks.

Pitt fretted about, intent to quell the crowd. He didn't notice as the Pastor reclaimed the pulpit.

Hiram stood, head bowed and in revered silence. His hands curled tightly about the wooden edge-work.

The silence spread. Even Pitt backed away without any of his signature prideful bluster.

"The Mayor is wrong. Sheriff Taylor did not just disappear," the Preacher revealed. "He asked me to go with him, and God forgive me that I didn't."

There were gasps and murmurings aplenty.

Hiram went on. "There are only three places Sheriff Taylor could have *disappeared*. On the way to the Circle Nine, On the way back from there, or...."

"Chose your next words carefully, Preacher," the Major boomed from the across the church. He raised his hand, a single finger pointing out a chastisement, but before the Major could continue, Pitt's teenage boy threw the church doors wide, letting a chill roll over the gathering.

Mayor Pitt's son was soaked but full of excitement. "It's him! He's busted out of jail and he's holed-up in Isaiah's livery."

"Meetings adjourned until our *new Sheriff* has dealt with this savage. Then we will reconvene at the Four Bits where drinks are on me!" The Major proclaimed. He smiled at his personal triumph and the young man's perfect timing. It was settled, leastways for now. Although he'd come up short of actually getting Franks duly elected as Sheriff, the spectacle of blood and beer would cut the edge from that. Besides, he knew none of the rest would take any action. Only actions mattered to the likes of the Major. Through force of character and intimidation the entire town was his.

There was some loud grumblings mixed in with the cheers as the Major, dressed in his uniform of far better quality than ever saw actual combat, led the town's leading citizens, and their wives, out into the storm. With the Preacher following his wayward flock.

The Major and his closest supporters stationed themselves directly across from the livery, on the Ambrose's boardwalk, while the rest spread out under storefront overhangs or any other place that afforded some protection from the wind and rain.

Mr. Franks looked to the Major, who gave him a slight nod. The gunhand got off his perch, stretched, and swaggered out into the street.

The Major's face grew into a victory smile as he flipped Franks the tin star of his new office.

The badge went ignored and landed in the mud behind him. The Major had bought his trigger, not his servitude. Franks turned his thoughts away from the Major. He spent a full minute, straightening his suit and getting into his professional mind set that was only interested in gore. There would be no attempt to disarm. No prisoner awaiting trial. Just trash spitting blood before collapsing into the mud.

"Hey Reb! I'm calling you out for the brutal murder of Mrs. Hertzig."

Most of the town was there, drifters included. The possibility of the town's first ever face-to-face shootout was captivating. Despite Eastern newspaper's romantic visions of heroic bloodshed and flying lead, this area hadn't seen this much action since before the war against General Antonio López de Santa Anna. That was all spittoon-talk though. No one remembered such violence around here. Back when these lands only supported a one shack, Texicano's pig farm.

"Scared?" he called out again. "You should be, I've seen your work. And you can't best me!"

The Major looked about the crowd. "Guess he isn't red. He's yellow!"

"You coming out? Or you-"

The stable door groaned inward and there he was. The stranger's left arm dangled lame. He had lost the Confederate shell jacket along the way and blood flowed through clenched fingers at his other side. The soldier had a Pocket model revolver jabbed into his belt and not one of those grapeshooters that he was so deadly skilled with. An unfamiliar pistol and half dead. A smile crept onto Franks' face. He had no idea what had happened to his enemy. Whether the Sheriff had stomped the snot from his prisoner or some of the Major's men had amused themselves. It didn't matter, either way it only made his job all the easier.

"And this time you ain't walking away from me." Franks squinted up at the sky. He cast about the crowd of onlookers, stepped up to a lady from the town meeting, yanked the parasol from her frightened grasp and as she recoiled, he tipped his hat.

Franks walked out into the street. "Weather like this could positively ruin a gentleman's hat."

The half-breed scraped himself forward. His face was tight, as if he was determined not to let the pain from his side show and not quite succeeding.

Lightning tickled the underside of a cloud bank.

The gunhand barked out a laugh. "Looks like there's not much left of you to kill."

Thunder rumbled as it swept over the town.

Franks was content to allow the other man do all the walking. He knew he was fast, too fast for the likes of the Indian-soldier. But a gun-fanner had to get up close enough to spit on the other man. With every step, the half-breed played more and more into his hand.

At twenty feet or so the Indian stopped, steadied himself into a statue and waited. The pain no longer showed.

The man was a soldier. And soldiers deal with pain well, Franks thought, but it wouldn't make him any less dead in a few seconds. He was flush with the knowledge that this gunfight would make his reputation in spades. People would be so stupid as to say that he had outdrawn a "gunslick" that had taken six men at once.

Twenty feet. Franks would have liked them to be still closer, but he didn't want any more mud than necessary on his boots.

There were no more words to be said. The two waited for one to make a move. Or a mistake.

In less than an instant, Franks knew that he'd won. Never had he pulled Nemesis so perfectly. Thought and action blended as one. Never had it felt so right. Unbeatable.

Nemesis tracked upwards, then betrayed him. Tumbled butt over barrel as it became more distant. Confusion was replaced by disbelief. His legs buckled and dropped him backwards into a sitting position in the muddy quagmire of the street. The parasol forgotten. His eyes confirmed what his mind denied. Air and blood bubbled out of the .41 caliber hole in his chest.

Morgan strode up and squatted. He unclenched his side and held the derringer before the professional-gun's face.

Franks' eyes widened with recognition. The son-of-a-bitch didn't beat his draw. He had cheated!

There was no resistance as the stingy pistol was forced barrel first into his mouth. He had been made to eat his words from when they first met, as well as the pistol. Gray eyes waxed over as his lifeless body collapsed backwards into the mud's embrace.

Mogan pulled out the blood-soaked meat from inside his shirt and placed it in the derby.

It hit the townsfolk. The wound in his side was as fake as lace curtains on an outhouse. But it gave a soldier a chance in a gunhand's game.

The hat landed upright at the Major's boots.

"You bushwhacked Franks and murdered Toby, you... you red-skinned son of a whore!"

The Pastor stepped in front of the Major, trying to calm him and was laid flat with a backhand that surprised most everyone. It was the Pastor who'd made everyone give up their guns before entering the church. If not, that damned heathen would already have air whistling through his head. And now, he had the grits to stand in the way? Oh hell no, Johannes thought.

"Once Buck gets here, he'll skin you alive. Then he'll get mean."

"Not going to happen," Morgan said with such quiet composure that it only burrowed deeper under the Major's skin.

"What the hell is that supposed to mean?"

"Buck can not."

"He damn sure can! I've seen him kill three of your betters with his bare hands. And this time he'll be ready for your evil, heathen ways." Veins bulged in his throat as his face twisted up ugly.

Johannes pulled himself up, a look of shock still tarred to his face.

Morgan looked him dead on. "Where do you think I got the liver?" He reached into the watch pocket of his pants, pulled out what he was after and tossed it into the derby.

Major Hertzig bent over and scooped up the hat. It took him a moment to realize what he was staring at. All the fire melted away and his eyes became lifeless. The thumbstall still laced around the severed digit.

It was then the Major realized that he was seconds away from death.

The half-breed had used the derby as a distraction and was coming for him . The pocket Colt held with grim purpose.

The Major knew any words would be useless. He was caught on open ground, and his Walker was still collecting church dust.

It wasn't like thirty years ago. Johannes was so secure up until a few moments ago. When he'd left the church steps, he had owned it all. Most every townsman owed him more than they'd ever earn off. A lighting fast killer as his personal Sheriff. There was nothing that he couldn't do.

But that was a few moments ago.

If Major Hertzig was trapped, it only made him more like a cornered Grizzly. Vicious and deadly.

But the townsfolk saw something else. It was only a touch, maybe not even that. Something akin to fear.

He made his move. Age and mud turned it into a lumbering hop, but it succeeded in putting the Pastor in the line of fire. Johannes had expected to be worm-fodder at first twitch, but he still knew that he didn't stand a Chinaman's chance unless....

The sword leapt free and came to a rest on Hiram's shoulder like a king investing knighthood. "One more step and the Preacher dies!"

The Major wasn't too surprised when the redskin came to a halt. He had figured it right. The injun was soft.

"Niles, give me your gun." Hertzig held out his free hand, fully expecting it to be filled.

But it was not.

"Conners." The Major called on those who owed him the most. "Pitt!"

Niles made sense, he was in debt past his eyeballs to Hertzig. It was as if he was looking at bags of free money if the Major fell.

Connors's face was ashen, horrified at what was happening. Though a businessman, he'd suckled at his momma's teat as she read the Bible.

Hertzig glanced about, hoping for others to step up. He was greeted with masks of bald-faced shock. Others simply would not return his gaze. The ungrateful bastards.

The Major's hand remained empty. Waiting there would only get him killed. He knew he had to retreat, to gather forces, before he'd ever own this town again. And it would take a full on storm of fire and bloodshed at that.

Johannes reached out and drew the Pastor towards him, turning Hiram to face the half-breed. The sword tracked inward also, until the Major held it in both hands, blade tight against his bullet-shield's throat.

"Pitt, have your boy fetch my horse," the Major ordered, "and be damn quick about it."

But the boy was rushing to do the Major's bidding without waiting for his dad's permission. Or approval.

It was a cold rain that owned the next few moments. The fight had ground into a muddy stalemate.

Jack and Alex came out from an alley next to the livery.

They sloshed their way up behind Morgan, who didn't take his concentration off the Major for an instant.

The Major's Big Grey was brought up alongside his owner.

Johannes noticed straightaway that someone had taken his rifle. He could've asked, but he knew none of the towners would speak up. That would all change on his return. Hell, he thought with a smile, they wouldn't just talk, they'd kiss his ass until it was chapped.

It was difficult, but the Major was able to mount without ever releasing his threat against the Pastor. For an old man, he was a well-skilled horseman. He grabbed the saddlehorn and dropped to one side of the horse's flank, giving his enemy nothing to shoot at but horse.

Morgan cocked the single action and took aim.

"No!" Jack yelled. "It'll blow your hand clean off!"

It had been Jack who fired away in the livery, overcome with rage at what Buck had done. He had slung lead twice until the pistol gave out a "popping" noise on the third pull, a telltale sign of a bullet stuck halfway down the barrel.

Morgan looked down at the Colt, switched it to his left hand, sighted a fine bead and pulled the trigger. The hammer struck the copper percussion cap and only made a sharp sputtering sound. Cap-and-ball's were more prone to the weather, old or bad powder or even just not enough measured grains behind the lead to throw it down range. Or it could've been Sal's neglect. Either way, The Major rode free.

Jack looked at him with disbelief, but glad his friend was still in one piece.

"Would you mind if I throw it at him?"

Morgan tossed the jammed Colt to Jack, who didn't know what to say. He caught the pistol and stood there, in the rain, staring at it, while Morgan made his way back to the livery.

Two of the stalls had been gutted out, walled off and converted into a smithy. Morgan may not have noticed except for the liveryman, who was face down in a water-filled slack tub. Unless the man had grown gills, there was no rush.

"Even you?"

Jack held the little boy's hand as they entered. Alex stood near his mom's body, but tried to act brave as he hurt worse than any boy should.

Morgan pulled the body from the red stained waters. Isaiah had put up a fight, the former slave's battered knuckles could testify to that. It was apparent that they had beat him, drowned him and probably would've blamed him for what happened to Sara. And not a soul left alive to say otherwise.

Morgan went over to Alexander.

"What will happen to me now?"

"I don't know," Morgan told the boy. "You will probably have to go and live with another family."

"No. I don't want to."

"What would you have me do?"

CHAPTER XVII

BAYONET INJUSTICE

It was on a false-Spring day, back in eighteen hundred and thirty-eight, when they came.

My father was an Englishman, turned Georgian farmer. My mother was a full-blooded, wise in the Old Ways, Cherokee. I am sure to outsiders they looked like an unlikely couple. But I saw the love and respect that they had for each other grow every single day. I was eight years old back then and blessed with the best of both worlds.

We had just sat down for dinner....

"Thank you, Lord, for the bountiful harvest that you have laid before us and for what you have in store for our future, whatever it may bring," my father prayed. They were so happy together. I had never seen my father so full of wonder as he placed his hand gently on my mother's large belly.

"He moved!"

"She."

They started to kiss, so it was left up to me to say "Amen" before I dug in.

We didn't have much. Nothing fancy. But no matter how thin things got, my parents made sure I never went hungry. A few times, my father was forced to sell one of his prized books, or two, for food. And when things got better, he'd always buy them back for a little bit more than he sold them for. Others would have given us food during the hard times, but my Dad was set against owing anything to anybody. No one who ever came to our door left hungry.

I loved my father, but when it came to farming, he would have been better off lecturing a crop instead of plowing, planting and harvesting it. He was not a big man, and farming was as foreign to him as teaching in London would have been to a Cherokee warrior.

Grandfather once told me that one time he had questioned my mother about her choice for a husband. He pointed out that my father struggled so when it came to hard labor. That the same tasks others could finish in less than half the time. He smiled at the memory and said she answered with two questions.

"Have you ever seen him do a job poorly, father?"

Grandfather could not say he had.

"Have you ever seen him give up?"

Grandfather said that he had thought on that question for days and he proudly told me that he never questioned her judgment again.

I was still remembering when a man crashed through our front door, lost his footing and both man and door hit the floor. His long-gun went off, but no one was struck by the bullet. The sound was trapped in our small cabin, adding to our fear.

Another man pushed his way past. He had a musket with a long spike bayonet leveled at my father.

This was the first time I had ever seen a bayonet. I knew of them from my father's nightly readings. I would go to sleep listening to Greek, Roman and, his favorite, English History.

My grandfather sometimes, when we were alone, would glance back over his life and tell me of the bayonets and cannons at New Orleans. But none of that prepared me for a foot and a half of sharpened steel leveled at my father.

We were forced outside, pulled by the hair, or shoved, or prodded, until we were clear of our house.

They wore no uniforms. And had no right to do this.

My father had told me that the highest court in America had ruled that we could keep the lands that were already ours. He told me how great America was, that differences could be settled by peaceful means. My father was a man of ideals. A man of peace. I still miss him.

They led us away, to the West, bayonets at the ready.

I could see a dozen or more columns of smoke rising from farms or outbuildings. The wind was fickle and brought with it the reek of destruction and death. There are no words, no turn of phrase, no language that can describe the sickly sweet smell of charred bodies.

Years later, that taste would come to me, unbidden, and shove me back to relive that day again and again. And after I woke, cold, soaked in sweat and uncertain, remembering that the nightmare was real, that is when I realized it was still trapped inside my head... and it will return again. It always returns.

Father was in the middle and held our hands. He squeezed mine so hard that my fingers turned pale, but I said nothing. I was trying to be brave.

The sun was setting and it hurt my eyes, but there was a horseman coming towards us. I could not make out much, other than he rode an immense white horse and was dragging something with a rope cinched to his saddle.

When we drew closer, I thought he was a Cherokee because it looked as if he wore a turban, but it was his linen shirt wrapped about his head and stained bright red with blood. It did little to staunch the stream of blood that coursed down his face and matted his chest-fur. He looked like a wildman. An evil spirit that had possessed a slain warrior. His eyes were huge and roved about, looking for something to kill.

Three of the armed militia approached. They tried to calm him. After seeing how hurt the rider was, one ran off to get a doctor while the other two tried to appease him with part of their loot. The first held up silver tableware and was ignored, while the other held up a quiver, with arrows and a bow strapped to it. A "prize of war".

The horseman dismissed it all with a backhand, knocking the quiver to the ground and sending them scurrying away.

He continued towards us. The bow made a loud snapping noise as it was crushed beneath the stallion's hooves.

As he approached, I could make out more details. Like the craftsmanship that went into the black and white braided horsehair rope that drug the body of what was left of a man.

Grandfather.

I ducked past the bayonet and ran to my grandfather's side. I had never seen someone so torn. He had been split open like a deer, half dressed, entrails loose and being pulled along. He was my hero. I would have given anything to save him.

I struggled with the rope until grandfather's ankle was free. The man on the horse ignored me as he reloaded a brace of dueling pistols.

Gently, I tried to scoop him up, clean the dirt from his insides and place them on top of him. I needed water, to purify him, because I knew he was dying.

Grandfather spoke to me in our ancestor's tongue. His voice never held such calm. Such kindness.

I started to cry. Silent tears. But I did not waste them. I used them to purify grandfather's face. It was a futile gesture, but it was meaningful.

He told me to take care of my mother and to live how he had taught me. He fumbled a gore covered wad of flesh and hair into my hand. He had taken a scalp before the horseman had claimed him.

I stuffed it into my pants pocket, to free up my hands. I still meant to help him as much as I could before he passed.

But I never had a chance as a hand crashed down on my head, curling into a claw about my hair and forcing me to my knees. The pistol jabbed hard against the back of my head. I was to be slaughtered. Alive, I was nothing to this man, but I was about to be used to torment my grandfather's last moments.

Kills-In-Water, warrior of the Wolf clan, focused his eyes on mine, smiled and he was gone. It was as if he had snapped his fingers and willed himself dead. In that instant, he robbed the horseman of his last taunt. And he took away my usefulness. It gave me a chance.

My father, who saw only that his son was being threatened, ordered the horseman to stop. My heart raced, I was useful as a pawn once again.

The horseman took his time, noisily drawing up a mouthful of spit and pelted grandfather's corpse, before turning his attention towards my father.

By my hair, I was lifted up, yanked about and brought in front of my father. The pistol barrel pressed harder.

"You call this one yours?"

"Yes," my father said with pride. "Morgan is my son."

"You admit to humping a squaw?"

My father didn't know how to take that. I could see the confusion on his face. His mouth hung open. For once in his life, he was at a loss for words. I don't think he had ever encountered such pure raging hatred before.

"You're a traitor to your kin." With that, I was forced back to my knees. The lock was drawn back. The sound was painful, but what was worse was that I could feel the mechanism click into place, transferred from the muzzle to my skull.

"Please," my father pleaded, "kill me instead."

Then the pistol was gone. But before I could understand why, I watched my father fall dead. Head-shot. The sound thundered inside me. I was stunned and crumbled, his hand still wrapped in my hair.

I was told not to worry, that he had another pistol.

Somewhere, far off, I heard my mother wailing.

Still bent forward, I opened my eyes to see the quiver the horseman had rejected. The bow was now broken, discarded and forgotten.

He raised me up and I was ready.

I gave the Devil a backhanded punch with all of my might.

The second pistol went off. I thought I was dead. My whole shoulder burned. I could smell the burnt flesh. The pistol-fire had killed all other noises, but I think I was screaming by then. I had never felt such pain.

With all of this, his grip loosened.

I dove for the quiver, grabbed out a second arrow, another bird-hunting flint point, spun and launched myself at him.

For his part, he was bewildered and only had time to look up from the switchcane arrowshaft that I had planted in his side.

We both crashed to the ground, him on his back and me still attaching like a rabid dog.

I was poised for the kill before he recovered his wits.

But I hesitated. For a second. Nothing more. It was not because of his eyes, so mad with hate that they seemed to brand me. Or because his shirt-turban had come off, revealing the bloody horror underneath. It was this man that Kills-In-Water had scalped. But I questioned myself to kill a man, in front of my mother. My father had taught me all of the "thou shall not's" from his Bible, and I was afraid of dishonoring him before his blood was even dry. Then I remembered grandfather's last words, for me to protect my mother....

I cocked back my arm and screamed as I brought down the razor sharp flint arrowhead for the kill.

Then blackness.

Then nothing more.

I was told later that a guard had come to the horseman's aid. That he had struck me with his musket barrel. That he had tried to shoot me, but he had forgotten that he'd fired his musket when he had lost his footing. That he had tried to reload, but my mother had bit him. Others had pulled her off of the militiaman, freeing him to barrel-slap me and save the horseman.

The horseman had survived, so I have heard. While he was carried to a doctor, I was carried to a stockade.

Politicians would label it a "camp," but it had little food, poor shelter, no outside medicines and they would kill anyone who tried to escape.

The horseman never appeared at the 'camp' or later on 'The Trail Where We Cried.'

I know.

I watched for him.

And I waited.

And I carried an arrow made for war.

I will not hesitate if I ever meet the one named Johannes Hertzig, Captain of Georgian Militia. Never again.

CHAPTER XVIII

MARRIAGE & OTHER THREATS

A crowd had gathered outside the livery and they were startled when the door was kicked open. Morgan came out, carrying Sara as gently as a newborn. She was draped in Morgan's gray shell jacket.

The townsfolk whispered back and forth when they saw her and the look on Morgan's face, but no one came forward to help. And no one got in his way.

Alexander appeared from the livery. He walked behind Morgan and his mother. His sleeves were tinted with blood, and he carried an unsheathed sword that seemed almost to glow of its own accord. It was a trick of the light and Isaiah's polishing that defied explanation.

The boy had pulled the sword from the bloody water barrel where Isaiah hid it when the Major's men had come to call. The same one that they drowned him in.

Lightning flashed, far off, but with a strength that made people duck or scurry for cover.

Hiram, still shaking from the ordeal, thanked the man who the day before wasn't good enough to set foot in his church. Yet even he stood well clear of Morgan.

Morgan walked past, as if he and Sara were alone, and up into the Ambrose.

The Pastor looked down at Alex, who was pushing on him.

"Come on, we need you."

He let himself be shoved along, and most of the town followed.

Hiram entered and saw Sara laid out on one of her own eating tables. Morgan was trying to arrange her to look like a sleeping princess of old. But the damage was done.

Hiram walked over next to the man. Tears went their way, neither hidden nor with a sound. The Pastor's hand balked. And again, but closer. Then he put it lightly on the sorrow-filled man's back.

"I'm so very sorry." Hiram said with thick regret. "There's nothing I can do." That wasn't quite true. He could start in on the last words, but Hiram knew that it wasn't the time. No one was ready for that yet.

"Marry us."

"What?" The Pastor said. "I... can't, she's gone."

They looked at each other. It lasted long enough for everyone assembled to notice. It wasn't a thing of intimidation, but the Pastor came away from it with a different understanding of this man. And later, he would reflect, of himself.

"Alrighty, everyone yank off your war bonnets and be amenable," Jack ordered. "My best friend's getting hitched!"

There was an awkward moment when the Pastor asked for her consent until Alexander, tears cascading down his chubby little cheeks, spoke up.

"She said, 'Yes.'"

The same three painted ladies whom Morgan had met earlier started up a hymnal.

Hiram was still struggling with his personal misgivings until he looked down to the boy's face. The face of innocence.

The Pastor didn't get three words out of his mouth before Morgan interrupted with a simple, "Yes."

"I now pronounce you man and wife," the Pastor said with a gentleness that had not been there in a long while. "You may kiss the bride."

"I am sorry," Morgan said, "I failed you."

He bent down and kissed her, his lips but a whisper of respect upon her warm supple lips. It lingered. Full of sorrow and unfulfilled dreams. As a first kiss should be and seldom is. Or as a last kiss never is, but should be.

It lasted until, slowly and unsteadily, she reached up and held his cheek as her lips caressed his in return.

There were gasps from the crowd. And more than a few cheers. Some looked to the Pastor as if he had just performed a God-honest miracle before their very eyes. While others were struck with the purity between the two. It was, for a moment, as if each person there was taken to another place. A place outside of the labors and concerns of the everyday. Outside of the Major's reign.

But it only lasted for a moment.

Years later, it was still argued if what they'd seen was a medical practicality or a bonafided miracle. No side ever won the argument, and no side ever truly lost.

The couple separated, so she could hold her baby-boy as if nothing else existed.

"I love you, Mommy," Alex said. Then grief overcame the boy, and he uncorked a bawling that would have wakened Saint Peter.

Time went by until Alexander calmed down enough to pull himself away.

Sara tried to speak, but only pain came out.

"You just rest," Morgan said in a sweet voice, "I must go and kill people now."

Alex held up the heavy Prussian-style, newly-reforged cavalry sabre.

"When you're done, you'll come back, right?"

Jack looked at Morgan. The man was awful busted up inside. But Jack knew that this man was a barrelful of grit and steel. Knew that he would never stop, would never give up and only dying could slow him down. But now he was asked to make a promise that no one could keep.

Morgan picked up a strip of blue silk and tied it to the sword's handguard. "I will kill all of those who hurt your mother."

"And come back, right?"

"Your mother needs you."

Sara watched the exchange. She still had her sense about her and reached out and drew her son to her, letting Morgan untangle himself from the boy's question.

They looked at each other, but there was nothing left to be said, so Morgan simply turned and walked away.

"Mr. Heathen, Sir?" Enos called from behind his station. "Sara left these with me, in case you came by. I think you'll be needing them now."

The hotel clerk brought up an arsenal from behind his counter. There were his matched Le Mats, a pair of Colt Dragoons still holstered in the pommelbags and one smaller .36 cal. hold out.

Jack had followed. "Geezus, You're packing kinda light, ain't you?"

Enos continued, placing the long mahogany case to the front of the pile.

"What were you before the war?" Morgan asked Jack.

"It might be hard to figure," Jack answered, "but I was a lawyer."

"Did you have any books?"

"Yeah, about a dozen. I was the best in my county." Jack looked at the finest sharpshooting rifle that he had ever seen. "What were you before?"

"I have always been a soldier." Morgan finished loading up and ripped a few unused pages from the ledger.

"You might could use this." Enos handed him the wooden signboard that had hung out front. It no longer barred Coloreds or Injuns, but had been crudely altered to read "No *Majors* or *other Scum* allowed."

"Thank you," Morgan told the old man.

"This still don't make us friends."

"Never said we were."

They shook hands.

Morgan went out on the boardwalk and Jack followed with the sign. Neither spoke for awhile. Jack stared out into the weather as his friend scribbled away.

The rain was steady now. A constant droning that calmed those who took a moment to just feel.

Jack pulled a little muslin sack of Durham from his vest, poured the fixings into a cornshuck and rolled out a quirly. He pulled a block of matches and snapped one off, struck it against the signboard and killed some tobacco.

He knew that there was no way of knowing who all was involved in attacking Sara. And even if there was, the others would throw in with their own. Twenty men? Two dozen? Maybe more? Then there was the Hertzigs, each deadlier than the next.

"Well?"

It took Morgan a moment before he finished and looked up.

"What do we do now?" Jack asked.

"I need your help to set up a few things."

"Anything you need, I'm your man." Jack took another pull. "Then what?"

"Can you take care of them for me?"

"I would rather stand 'side you."

"I know. That is why I can trust you to look after them."

"Ok," Jack said, "I will." There was a new forged resolve in his manner that had replaced the hollow promise of opium. For the first time since the war, he felt alive. He looked back out over the rain before changing the subject.

"You have any idea what you're going up against?"

"Yes." Morgan ripped out a couple of pages, stood up and joined Jack's weather gazing. "That's why I need you to take care of them."

xXx

Justine Hertzig had left the Circle Nine shortly after her father had gone into town. She was nervous, more so than ever before in her life. But this was the opportunity she had waited for since her thirteenth birthday. The plan wasn't bred from a place of hope, but from the seething hate of her past. And her "now." For all she'd done for her daddy, he was ungrateful. He had bought her silks and cosmetics, but he made it clear that she would never inherit. Would never own what she'd earned hundreds of times.

She would make this run with a horse no one would miss, gear that no one knew she had and a desperate need to escape the nightmare it was to be a 'Hertzig.' She had taken everything money, jewelry and all the papers, deeds from her father's safe. She'd torn the library apart and left a crude note, framing the Indian-stranger for what she'd done, figuring that it just might buy her enough time to escape. Justine had rounded the horn and she knew it full-well, afraid even to speculate what punishments awaited her for such betrayal. To be able to provide for her new family governed her timing more than her fears dominated her.

When she arrived in Calvary, it was more ghost town than anything else. Most would be at the church, listening to her father's grand decree.

Justine had bought a stagecoach ticket with twenty-seven minutes to spare. Owing to the mud, she figured, she still would have less than an hour to wait.

One hour until freedom.

She stayed inside Cartman's and idled the time away. Justine had bought the ticket there, and staying put gave her a chance to dry out a bit. Plus, she figured, the fewer people who saw her the better.

Justine idled away the time, scything through the bolts of cloth as if they were chaff. She acted somewhat interested in a few of them before she discarded each one with a flip or a toss or just let them drop from her fingers.

"Worthless, worthless, worthless," Justine told no one but herself.

Mr. Cartman had been through this many times. She wasn't actually yelling or breaking things, so he was grateful that she was so well disposed today.

All of his regulars had learned to hightail it once the Major's daughter entered and would not come back until she was long gone. So when the small bell mounted on a pigtail spring above the door announced a new customer, both the shopkeeper and his only customer were taken aback.

The 'waltzing-barbarian' entered the store. Soaked. An old grain sack in one hand and a saber, carried by the sheath, in the other. If the new customer was surprised to see her, Justine was a downright unbeliever.

She knew he was dead. Certain of it as she was of her own name. No one could survive the rattlesnake's poison and Sal's cruelty. Fear drove Justine to trust her eyes as he strode towards her. She was able to get the derringer from her purse, to raise it and collapse. The loud hollow clonk still hung in the air as Cartman laid her out flatter than a sheet of paper. The little shopkeeper stood there apologizing to the unconscious lady. The cast iron skillet clutched in both of his trembling hands.

Morgan stepped over Justine, as if skillets and ladies' noggins were commonplace in his world. He pulled a slip of ledger-paper from his vest pocket, "I need some supplies."

Business scrubbed the shock off the storekeeper. "By the look of things, I can give you anything but a cup of water," Cartman smiled at his own joke, but it fell flat.

"I have no money," Morgan said with a concerned look on his face.

"Then why should I get any more involved against the Major?"

"They left Sara broken. Isaiah and the Sheriff are dead."

"I am sorry. I heard the Sheriff was missing, but nothing of the others," Cartman said, "but as a businessman, I can't afford to take sides in something like this."

"I am not talking to a businessman," Morgan said, his voice quiet but thick with emotion, "I am talking to a man."

Those words lingered between them. Cartman could feel the other man's hurt. It was one thing not to stop a killing inside your store, but to side against the Major was the same as carving the dates into your own headstone.

Cartman pinched the bridge of his nose, eyes squeezed shut. It did not matter if this stranger didn't have a single chance, Cartman thought. Sheriff Taylor, Isaiah and Sara were good people. And now there was a man willing to take up the sword against such a powerful evil. How could he, as a simple man of faith, not help such a man? Without another word, the little man took the paper, unfolded it and scanned the list of supplies.

"You'll need to borrow my wagon to carry all of this."

"No. I need you to deliver them," Morgan said as he pulled out another paper. "I wrote out some instructions."

"You know that no one will stand with you?"

"You are."

Mr. Cartman shook his head, both at the man's truth-filled words and at the odd assortment of supplies. "Some nails? Who are you going to crucify?"

"A couple of snakes," Morgan said as he picked up his sack and made to leave.

"Wait. You know that the Major's men did this?" The storekeeper turned his purpled and swollen face to give the outsider a full view.

"Yes."

"And they took whatever they wanted?"

Morgan's eyes were still bloodshot from his silent tears shed for Sara. All he could do to reply was a single nod.

"So why did you ask, instead of just take?"

"For the same reason you are helping me." He opened the door and the brass bell rang anew.

"Wait."

Morgan paused and looked back, but kept hold of the doorknob.

"You know, the paper on sticks of dynamite isn't red, it's tan."

"No I didn't," Morgan answered, "but neither did they."

"I have something that might help you. It's in the back. Come, see for yourself."

The bell rang again as Morgan shut the door and he followed the shopkeeper.

xXx

Morgan left Cartman's and was well on his way to the town's only bank when he was cut off.

The cream of Calvary approached, hats in hand and clumped too close together. They had the Preacher with them, to stiffen their resolve or possibly for protection. Desperation had driven them to this. Each one of them had a different image of what the Major would unleash upon the town. Having their town burnt to a cinder was not their idea of good business.

They came to a stop in front of him. Too far away for idle conversation, yet far enough to get a head start if they had to run. One stepped forward, intent to be their spokesman, but at a complete loss for how to address the stranger. He looked about as comfortable as a man with a hatful of chiggers stuffed down his britches.

He made to get to speachifying when Morgan motioned them to wait. And they did.

Pastor Hiram Evander, Bible in hand, stepped in front of the bank doors.

"I can not let you hurt this man," he said. Everyone knew that the Banker was a steadfast Hertzig supporter, but his calling was above all of that.

Morgan sat down the burlap sack and pulled out a yellow-handled straight razor.

"Do not worry," Morgan said. He looked past the clergyman and smiled.

Hiram followed his gaze. A fly had taken refuge from the incoming storm on a wooden post. Sluggish from the weather, Morgan neatly sliced it in two. The half-Cherokee caught the fly's remains in his off hand.

"Once inside, I will not hurt a fly."

"Swear that on the Bible."

Morgan stopped again, turned and looked the Pastor dead on. "I never lie."

With unmatched smugness, Stewart Ellsworth peered over his gold-rimmed spectacles at the most unlikely pair he had ever seen anywhere, much less right outside his bank. But only the penniless savage entered. Stewart made an odd nasally disrespectful sound and went back to arranging a new stack of foreclosures.

Mr. Ellsworth was a particular fellow in about every way that mattered. His salt and pepper hair grew in splotches, but only from the ears down. What it lacked in coverage, was made up for in length. He wasn't trying to compensate for the barrens north of his eyebrows, but he just considered both barbers and dentists a frivolous expenditure.

His wardrobe consisted of two suits, both of which he'd bought from a widow selling her deceased husband's effects. Neither fit his angular frame, nor smelled quite right and were of a style that no one, short of some ungodly huge bribe, would admit to liking.

But for all of that, he had thousands of friends. And six times a week, right before closing the vault, he would wish them all a good night.

The banker was quite offended when the savage pushed through the hip-high gate and made his way to a chair across from him.

"You have no account here and I am not in thee business of handouts," Elsworth said, "so we have nothing to discuss."

"I am not here to have a discussion." He looked out the big front pane, and the banker's eyes followed his lead.

Stewart saw them there, Calvary's finest, hats in hand and looking like somebody had just died. Or was about to.

"You can't threaten me."

The Pastor had his face squished up against the front door, peering in. He held the Bible up for those inside to see.

Stewart turned his attention back to the intruder and was shocked to see him holding a straight razor and his eyes circling about in an odd little pattern.

He struck. Without warning. Coming deathly close to the banker as he made the blade skip. And it was done. Before the banker could do more than fear for his life, the shaving knife returned to his vest pocket.

The savage reached over and took Elsworth's white linen handkerchief and placed it on the desk, picking up something off the desktop that the banker hadn't noticed before.

At the linen's center was half a fly, still twitching. He had never seen such a feat. Or anything even a close second. As he looked up, the man plucked the other half from Stewart's shoulder.

"How... how?"

"I will have all of Hertzig's money now."

Elsworth had never been robbed. He might be a lot of things, but he felt it his duty, no matter how scared, to protect the money entrusted to him.

"No."

"Do not move." The razor reappeared. His eyes seemed transfixed on the banker's receded hairline. "I hate lice."

Morgan came out of the bank, weighed down considerably by the oversized and overstuffed leather and canvas bank-bag he now carried along with his original burlap sack.

The same spokesman stepped forward once again.

"No."

"But mister," the spokesman looked back over his shoulder for support, "you haven't even heard what we have to say."

"Yes, I have," Morgan told them as he kept walking, "dozens of times."

They had more to say, a lot more. And they thought their offer a damned fair one. More importantly, they felt it was their only chance of saving their town. They needed him.

"I'll go get the United States Cavalry if you don't listen to our offer," the spokesman called after him. The Sheriff's badge and towner's offer went unseen and unheard.

"More than likely, you already have."

CHAPTER XIX

THE RECKONING

The Four Bits batwing doors opened slowly, revealing Morgan, but not like any of the towners had ever seen him before.

He was bristling with handguns and wore a sword strapped across his back like some particularly bloodthirsty bandido would wear a machete.

All conversations and ballyhoo ended. Even the blind pianoman held off. People scrambled out of the way, scared that they'd be caught between the stranger and whomever he had come to kill.

"Company, ladies," Señora Isabella said as she came forward, trying to restore the atmosphere.

"Well, well, well," she pulled her working voice out of storage. "And to what do I owe this pleasure?"

"Name your price."

She twirled a loose strand of hair. "Aren't you freshly married?"

"I meant for the Four Bits."

"Unlike most things you see here, it's not for sale."

"Today, it is."

"Now, I wonder, what would a man like you would need with a place like this?"

He smiled. It was a fierce thing. One that could only add up to more hurt to the Major.

"Your smile says the most interesting things. Come, step into my office said the spider to the fly."

"All right, but which of us is the spider?"

Isabella had a good laugh as she led the way.

xXx

Jack waited outside the Four Bits as it drained of customers and entertainment alike. It had been a long time since he had handled a buckboard. Or felt the rain.

Morgan and Isabella were the last out.

Jack forgot himself, stood up and almost fell flat. He gripped the reins, awkwardly regained his balance and whipped off his hat. "Miss de Anza."

She held her laugh down to a smile, but it wasn't easy.

Morgan tossed the bank-bag into the wagon bed, landing next to the long mahogany box and the altered signboard.

"There is more than enough to buy everything you need. Split the rest between you and Mr. Cartman."

Morgan jumped up onto the wagon seat. "I almost forgot," he said to the Madam, "may I have three more tokens?"

An odd request from a newly married man, Isabella thought. A man living on borrowed time. "I'll leave them on top of the bar, but now you owe me three dollars, so don't go getting yourself killed until you pay up."

Morgan counted out three more dollars and handed it to her. She understood.

"You have the heart of a conquistador. Why don't you take your woman and just ride. Ride and never ever look back," she said, wishing that such a man would ride into her life.

Morgan tipped his hat to the lady. "It has been a pleasure."

"No, but it could have been."

"Where we going now?" Jack asked.

"To the livery."

"Again?" But Jack was already turning the team. "Then what?"

Morgan handed him a second sheet of instructions. As Jack read, he started to laugh. "You know that the War is over, right?"

"No," Morgan said in a toneless voice, "but it will be soon."

"I'll need a heck of a lotta help to set this all up. Plus, it'll probably take all night to do."

"I know," Morgan told him, "that is why I must go out and pay the Major a social call."

xXx

"...and then, I swear to God, he cut the fly in two." Stewart Ellsworth told them. But the Major, two of his men and a third one, one that looked like filth and pistols, seemed even more skeptical at the second telling.

Longhorn and Dogbite held their tongues. The story was too farfetched to be real, but the banker had never been known for a storyteller, or a drinker, or as anything else that'd throw off his mind enough to make up such a thing.

But the other man cut out a snort. "If it was my money, I'd slice him thin and fry him in grease." He pointed a thumb at the banker.

"Silas here don't believe you," the Major said. His tone was sweeter than sugar on honey, and scared Ellsworth all the more.

The Major continued, but the banker didn't catch it. His mind was stuck on that name... Silas. Silas Donathan. He had heard stories, vicious stories. Where Mr. Franks would do horrors for profit, Silas would do worse for fun, or for no reason at all.

"What?"

"I said you're a lucky man."

"I... I don't see how?" Ellsworth said as he sopped up his face sweat.

"Because I'm a born forgiver," the Major said. Although his tone was dripping with sweetness, it failed to convince anyone, a failure which made the banker tremble and redoubled his impression of taking a shower on the spot.

"I could always give you all the town's money, and tell them that the Indian stole everything?"

"That won't cover my losses."

"But that'll make everyone fall deeper into your debt. And when you kill him, you'll nearly double your money." Ellsworth felt pride at his fast accounting solution.

"So I should let you live?"

The loyal banker was shot full of stupid. He didn't realize that he was bargaining for his life. Suddenly, he felt afflicted, looking like a field mouse who had just woken in a den of snakes.

The Major laughed as he led the banker out of his home. He profoundly apologized for poking fun. But when the Major patted him on the back, Stewart cringed away.

Stewart hurried to get going, stumbling up into the buggy and grabbing at the reins as a drowning man grabs at a chance for life.

"I'll send two of my men by in the morning for my money," the Major said as he smiled and waved.

Ellsworth didn't hesitate, didn't return the wave and never looked back.

xXx

It was late, real late. Or too early, depending how open a man's eyes were. Unless Mexicans or hostiles were beating on the main gate, Corporal Osburn felt that the time between the bugle calls was his... unless he was pulling duty. He could hear some Private running about like a chicken with his head cut off and running out of places to look. Footfalls told him that he was found out. The rapid banging on the outhouse's door interrupted Osburn's mission.

"Corporal? Corporal Osburn? Are you in there?"

"What?"

"The Lieutenant wants to see you right away!"

"Dammit," the big Irishman said, "tell him I have to finish wiping my ass before I can wipe his."

The young Private started off, then stopped, not sure if the newly assigned two-striper was yanking his lanyard or not. He mulled it over quickly and decided that he should edit the Corporal's reply.

It was a small post. On paper, it was manned by a full Company, but paper has a way of lying like an unhappy lover. The entire command numbered twenty-one. But the boots to stirrups number was eighteen at present, with two medically unfit for duty. And there was Sergeant Graves, the senior enlisted man, awaiting a Regimental Court-Martial for embezzling, assault and indecent behavior at a divine service.

Osburn entered the Commanding Officer's office a few minutes later. The air held a gray thickness from the Long Nines that the Lieutenant and a civilian were smoking.

"Yes, Sir?" he said with most of a salute.

"Did you knock?"

"ah... no?"

"Try again."

He banged at the door, rapidly and with such force as to wake the garrison. And he entered, without waiting to be told or asked *who* it was.

"Corporal Osburn reporting as ordered, Sir," he roared louder still, but this time his salute was straight out of the manual.

The Lieutenant looked up as he put his watch back in his vest pocket. "Corporal, this is Mr. Pitt. He's the Mayor of Calvary."

They shook hands and the Lieutenant continued. His eyes sparkled with yet-to-earn medals. "There's this old military man, a Mr. Hurtshog and some Indian, that's stirring up some trouble and the entire town is pleading for me to save it!"

"Beggin' your pardon Sir, but ain't this a matter for the Sheriff?"

If looks could, the Lieutenant's would have slain the entire Irish Brigade. "I want a full kit inspection one hour after Reveille. Directly after which, we ride to Calvary." Lt. Kilpatrick's eyes focused on some other place. Some other time. "Leave two men to maintain the Post.

"Anything else, Sir?"

"No, no, that'll be all, Corporal."

Osburn popped to attention and saluted. And held it. But instead of returning the protocol, the Officer slowly worked his pocket watch back out, still working the cigar.

The salute became stale, but remained.

"Oh, Corporal, one last thing," the Lieutenant said, "thirteen minutes is unacceptable." He exhaled a long column of smoke at the hanging oil lamp.

"Sir?" The enlisted man was so clearly lost that the officer explained.

"Yes, the time it took you to report. I will not tolerate sloth or a lack of military deportment in my command. We'll just have to work on that upon our return, won't we Corporal?" He returned a quick, dismissive salute as he finished speaking.

The last of it was put as a question. As if Osburn would have any choice. He could tell the Lieutenant that he was burying Quakers, but it wouldn't matter. There was probably a manual somewhere that regulated the time, the placement and even the proper clean-up operation. And if anyone in the whole United States Army had a copy, it would be Lieutenant Kilpatrick. Hell, the bastard probably wrote it. There was only one thing for Osburn to do.

"Yes, Sir," the Corporal agreed.

xXx

There was much drinking, laughter and goings-on inside the Circle Nine's bunkhouse. With the Sheriff's death and the defilement of the little peach slice from the Ambrose, their whole world had changed overnight. Now they'd be able to ride into Calvary anytime the wished, take whatever they desired, and leave nothing behind but fear. They had been elevated from plantation overseers to masters of the entire county. And that was just the beginning.

"When's Sal coming back?" said Bugeye. He squinted now, like a groundhog. His glasses a casualty of Sara's wrath.

"Who cares," Hoyt said, "I'm just glad he went to kill that *SumBitch*."

The others all laughed at the last of it, an overblown impersonation of Longhorn.

The door was pounded on three distinct times.

The laughter died off. "Who the hell's there?"

"It's me, the redskinned *sumbitch*."

Laughter exploded from within. It was the God-awfulest Longhorn sound-alike try they had ever heard. "What'dya want?"

The banging grew loader and more insistant.

"Hold up, I'm a'coming," Critter, his cheek still weeping blood from Sara's fingernailing, opened the door. "Sal?"

A scream came from deep within his insides. It was filled with fear and a need to run. To run fast. So fast that somehow the big ivory handled Bowie knife wedged into his guts would no longer be there. He backpedaled, out of control, until he fell down, legs still racing to get him away from the pain. The scream dwindled into a sobbing chant.

"Oh God, Oh God, oh God... ohGod."

An old grain sack flew in from the open doorway and landed between Critter's legs. Some of the contents became annoyed and started in on a rattling jamboree. Slowly, one slid his thick diamond-shaped head out, forked tongue flickering. The newly spiritual man

. L. Woods

froze as he gawked at the movement between his legs. "Ooh god."

One of the men used his rifle to shut the front door, not willing to expose himself any further. Others ran about, grabbing their longarms, gunbelts, or whatever they could find to hold off this one-man assault.

Without his spectacles now, Bugeye looked more the part of a groundhog as he popped his head out the front window anyway. It was a quick thing, a poor balance between a need to know what was going on and not getting the top of his head blown off.

"What did you see?"

"Cain't see nary a soul anywheres," Bugeye whispered.

"No shit? Squint harder."

"Hey, Indian," Hoyt yelled. "You got Critter. Fair enough. But you're going to half'ta come inside to kill all of us!"

"Hoyt." Critter said in a scared little voice.

"Ain't nothing out there but a sword stuck in the ground," Bugeye told Hoyt. "And there's something flapping from it."

"Hoyt?"

But Hoyt paid his friend no heed, figuring that Critter was a dead man trying to spout mushy crap about nothing while what was going on outside was life and death for everyone else.

"Well, what the hell is it?"

"I dunno. Something black. No, no, I think it's blue."

"Blue?" Hoyt knew now that they had stuck their peckers in a beehive.

"Hoyt!"

"What!"

"The bag is smoking."

Hoyt looked over his shoulder and saw smoke wisping from within the course-woven burlap. The room went silent, so silent that all could actually hear the fuse burning.

"Oh sh-"

xXx

The plantation wasn't through shuddering from the explosion when Wesley shot out the double glass doors that lead to the backyard. He had hunkered low and zigged, rifle at the ready, until he got to a low stone wall that separated the terrace from the rest of the Major's lands.

The former Infantry Officer didn't stand up until he found a big enough shadow to do so, painfully aware of how much the moonlight on a two-story white building would outline him.

He couldn't see exactly what had occurred, but from the direction of the flames and what screaming there was, Wesley knew that the bunkhouse was no more.

"Round up everyone still breathing. No one sleeps until we kill him, you make that damn clear," the Major told Wesley.

"Father?"

The Major looked down upon his son.

"You'd better get back inside," Wesley said as he squeezed his frustration out on the Winchester. "before you get shot."

"You better be damn sure you know what you're doing, boy," the Major declared. "'Cause a week ago you'd have crapped yourself before squaring off with me."

But Wesley was beyond caring about his father's scorn. "Last week you hadn't ordered Sara to be attacked."

"You mean last week when she loved you?"

"Yes!" His yell was a anguished thing.

"Did you ever wonder why she asked you to marry her?"

"Or why she was crying when she asked you?"

"Or why she's always busy when you come to call?"

Wesley couldn't answer.

"She never was yours," his father went on. "That no-account husband of hers left her nothing but a mountain of debt and the startings of a litter. So I, *I*, paid off every marker, without her knowing, and then I had a chat with her. And guess what? She'd rather marry you than work on her back or beg in the streets."

"No..." It came out as a plea. For it not to be true. Or at least for his father to stop.

"I fixed it so you could marry the girl you been sweet on for years and this is the gratitude I get? Damn boy, you'd better put down that rifle and start apologizing or you'd better start shooting."

Wesley was caught within himself and could not figure out how to go on.

"Well which will it be?"

Wesley gently laid the rifle on the cold wet grass.

"I hate you."

"I know." The Major started back inside. "Now go and find your sister and tell her it's time for bed."

Chapter XX

Under the Black Flag

It was shortly after breakfast when the Major's men rode in to Calvary. In pairs and scouting. All grim-set and wound up.

Two were cut to pieces as they tried to enter the Four Bits. One grapeshot from each of the LeMat's under-barrel saw to that. And the other scouts had their answer.

After some confusion, all but one took up good firing angles on the whorehouse, while the one went back to report to the Major.

The Major led the long column of men into the town. They entered from the East, using the town as cover.

Major Johannes Hertzig looked all the part of a conquering noble, upon his big gray and dressed in his very best Sunday-go-to-church uniform.

Silas rode beside him. He wore nothing fancy. Or anything clean. Instead of garnish and a sword, he wore pistols. A lot of pistols. With his horse carrying his back-ups.

Behind those two, Wesley and a young man bearing a standard that had never been flown in these parts.

The black flag was the symbol of bushwhackers. Bloody irregulars that swooped down without warning, using pistol and scatterguns, and leaving before the Federals had a chance to hitch up their pants. They tried to cover pillaging, rape and murder under that small patch of black fabric.

Today, it meant no quarter. Only death.

The better part of two other crews had also thrown in with the Major. Most of the evil in four counties. Whether for money, for debts unknown, or for glory, they were there.

Near three dozen in all.

The heart went out of the townsfolk. There was no way the half-breed could hold out until the Cavalry arrived. Nothing to stem the Major from exacting his retribution on them.

The streets seemed as if they hadn't been used in years. Even the stray dogs had enough sense to tuck tail.

The Major sat noble upon his big gray with Silas next to him, carbine in hand and ready for war.

They pulled up between the Ambrose and Isaiah's livery.

Buck met them first. He was naked, save for a barrel tied about his mid-section, and slowly twisted from the livery's freight pulley.

The sign that had, until recently, hung outside the Ambrose was now posted to the livery's door. To the Major it was as much of a challenge as his son's lifeless body curing twenty feet above the street.

Wesley didn't wait for his father and took three men with him to see to his brother. They broke through the bolted door and disappeared inside.

"Major?" It was Hiram Evander, the Preacher, in simpler clothes than anyone had seen him wearing in years.

"There's no need to harm anyone... he's waiting for you at the Four Bits."

The Major made to answer when an avalanche of wood, metal and movement came from within the livery as Buck's body smashed the ground. A cloud of dust, dirt and hay rolled outward from the doorway. Pitiful calls for help and of pain followed.

Silas and others crept inside and were stuck with what they saw. Men crushed or speared. Dead or dying. A mound of farm tools and blacksmith equipment had half buried one of the men. Another was laying in horseshit and wailing. Only Wesley was still standing, but he looked like he'd just swallowed a scorpion.

It was a simple trap. As they had lowered Buck, a second rope, tied to the first that none had seen in the darkness of the loft, pulled a pre-weakened four by four. When the wooden post snapped, it released a wagonbed-full of sharp metal and heavy iron.

Braced and holding the first rope, they never had a chance. And it wasn't over. Not for Wesley and the wailing man.

Long nails through thin boards, pointing up. Concealed under a layer of horsemuck, the boards had been placed where one would jump, or dive to, while trying to survive a man-made avalanche.

They carried Wesley out, both feet still pinned to a board.

"He got my tallywacker," the other wailed, drool streaming from his eyes, nose and mouth. Helpless as the day he was squirted into the world.

Silas laughed and went back outside. Others would help the injured man. Or not.

They took over the church. Immediately smashing out firing ports in the stained glass windows along the side facing the Four Bits.

A single shot rang out and one of Silas's men was done in. And it changed everything.

The Major and Silas argued. Two leaders, neither wanting to follow the other. Or agree to the other's plan. They became two separate commands.

Silas was happy now, in his element as he readied his men. And he would no longer owe the Major for his ranch. They cinched down their saddles and checked their pistols. No words were said. It was a time for each man to steel himself for what came next.

"Hell, if it keeps raining like this, I'll have to take a bath just to dry out a bit," Silas told his men, trying to break the tension.

"A thousand dollars to the man that brings me his head." That had a better effect, he could see smiles now.

They rounded the church at a gallop, all war whoops and rebel yells. pistols firing at nothing. It was a terrible thing to behold. Especially if the defender was a greenhorn Unionist.

But this wasn't that war. And Morgan was anything but a greenhorn. The world itself had changed.

From the church, the Major's men tried to lay a covering volley, but the horsemen rode between the two buildings, cutting off their support.

The mud slowed their horses and a wall of lead ended it.

One man, three Winchesters and forty-five well placed shots, fired as fast as one could lever. More than half were dead. Some from the bullets, but almost as deadly was when sixteen hundred pounds of horseflesh decides to catch their death and tumble. Some carried away bullets or broken bones. Others hid behind a downed horse. Bits of white cloth sprouted like weeds, frantically flapping, desperate to avoid catching a mean case of lead poisoning.

Those who tossed their weapons and turned spurs were allowed safe passage, unless they tried for the church.

Only the young man with the flag was still mounted. He had stopped in the middle of it all. Unsure of what to do.

"That Indian must be out of ammo," one of them yelled, but he wasn't willing to test out his own belief.

Another peeked out and was rewarded with a new hair style. A permanent one.

Those in the church were not exactly certain of the sharpshooter's location. The charge that had cut off their line of fire also obstructed their line of sight. Others were too busy forting up their own positions. And some preferred just to watch the carnage.

But now they returned fire with a vengeance. Hundreds, then thousands, of rounds were put into the windows and building front. Anyplace that could hide a man with a rifle. Each bullet stinging away. A few planks fell free. But the building weathered the assault like an old whore, badly used, but still serviceable.

Silas Donathan used the slinging lead to high-tail it for the church and died. A single shot to his face.

"Cease fire." The Major ordered as he put away his Walker. It was more to take command of the men than to stop firing. Most had already burned through all their rifle ammo.

A few of them started yelling and cussing at the flagbearer, trying to get him back to the church. He looked back at them, smiled with the bravo that only youth, or dementedness, can claim and he charged.

A single shot echoed out and he tumbled, feet skywards, off the back of his horse. His prized flag thrust into the ground. The soaked banner hung limply now. Not even the harsh wind made much of a difference.

The men grew sullen. Some who had lived through the charge had not returned. Leaving Calvary behind and not looking back.

Another shot rang out. And their standard was no more. He had splintered the ash pole in a single shot.

Wesley had noticed. The shot had a deeper report. Not like the Winchesters.

"Wesley."

"Yes, father?"

"Come here and tell me what you see."

His son used a rifle as a crutch, but he suffered to get to his father's side.

The Major had been watching the action through his old service binoculars.

"What do you see, at the windows."

Wesley did so. "I'm not sure... it looks like we've chipped away the shadows.

"Damn!" The Major took back the field glasses. "That's what I thought."

Wesley was amazed. The brothel had been turned into a fortress overnight. Inset from the windows was wooden armor, painted or tarred to resemble a darkened interior. It meant that he probably would be firing at them, killing them, from small gun-slits. Perhaps not even from the windows, but from cut-outs that resembled a loose plank. Wesley realized that for all their gunfire, they may have only improved his concealment. And there was the question of the bigger rifle that could strike where he willied it to.

The Major centered himself in the church. "Alright boys, listen up. I want you six to go get supplies. Longhorn, you're in charge. Get sacks of grain, barrels, nails. Whatever else you can think of. And get every gun, every bullet and all the powder that this town has. I'll pay up once this all is settled."

The Major pointed to two of Silas' men, I want you to sneak around and find a backway in, or just shoot him from a window."

"Get medicine and bandages," Wesley interrupted, "and see about getting the Doc in here."

"And food," Dogbite called.

The Major pulled a pure white cloth from a table, knocking the religious trappings on to the floor.

"Dogbite."

"Yes, Major."

"I want you to go out there and talk to him," the Major said, tossing the white linen at him.

"Me, Sir?"

"As long as you are under a flag of truce, he will honor it."

"It's not like you to surrender, Father," Wesley ribbed. He knew that his father would trade all of their lives before he'd ever surrender. It just wasn't in his blood.

They went to their taskings. Dogbite, the most reluctant of all.

Dogbite let as much time as he could get away with before setting out with his white flag. He made it all but about sixty yards before a shot struck the water in front of him.

"Heyheyhey." Dogbite said, holding the flag like a shield. He waited, trying to figure out where the half-breed was watching him from. But his feet remained anchored in place. Too many had died to risk a step. Time drug on, making Dogbite more and more nervous. He turned back towards the church and tried to gesture his lack of understanding.

"What do you want?"

"You're going to die here. In a few minutes, or in a few hours. We have enough of those newfangled Winchesters to outfit an entire company. They ken fire enough lead to kill a thousand men."

"Maybe. But I live now."

Damned mule-head Injun, Dogbite thought. He'd never met someone so willing to fill a coffin. This powwow wasn't going near where he had thought it would.

"I'm here to offer you another option." He waited for that to sink in. "All ya gotta do is put down your weapons and surrender."

"You tell the Major," Morgan said, "come and take them."

Dogbite shook his head. "How much would it cost for you to leave and never come back."

"Come closer."

Dogbite did so. He hated all of this. He was the bully, and he was supposed to tell others what to do. But there was no arguing with the Major. It was unhealthy.

"Closer."

He did this also.

"Your knuckles are tore up."

"Yeah, so?"

"You were in the livery." It was not a question.

The bastard came into view, standing within the half-shadows of the entranceway.

Dogbite fixed a plan in his head. If he could just drop flat, they could shoot him dead certain. But, his mind raced on, if they miss he was a dead man. Or if they shot and hit him, he'd be just as dead.

The bastard held a worn-out pair of war issue lace-ups in one hand, dropped half a handful of gold coins into each and placed them down in the entranceway and without taking his eyes from Dogbite, disappeared back into the Four Bits.

Dogbite had sneaked a pistol, but to grab, cock and aim would have taken longer than he would have lived. Besides, he was no hero. And now there was gold.

The negotiator advanced. Still worried that a bullet would come from within. But, he reasoned, if the bastard had wanted him dead, he would've been taking a mud nap a hundred yards back.

"What the hell am I supposed to do with those?"

"Give them to your Master," Morgan said. "It is my answer."

They were tied together and Dogbite used the laces as a handle.

"Oh, by the way. You know we 'invited' some of the regular folk to help us fort up?" He said over his shoulder. "And they'll be staying with us until this here thing is settled."

Dogbite made it back to the church with only the slick mud giving him any further troubles. He walked up to the Major.

"I told him we took some townsfolk prisoners, so he won't try to blow us up or something."

"Great," Wesley said, "that means he's just going to take that much better aim."

"I was told to give you these," Dogbite said to the Major. He held the shoes by the soles, as if he was returning with a holy relic.

"What do they mean, Father?" Wesley asked.

"That's Injun symbolism," the Major said as he dismissed Dogbite with a shooing gesture. "It means he doesn't need them anymore. He's not going anywhere."

"Is that what we truly want, Father?"

"It's exactly what we want."

Wesley was not so sure. The stranger had only met hate, jail and more hate since he entered town. He could have pulled up stakes, had plenty of opportunity, yet here he was. Four years of warfare had taught Wesley not to fight a well-emplaced, well-seasoned enemy on ground of his own choosing.

"And the money?" Wesley asked.

"What?"

"I saw him drop coins into the shoes, through my field glasses."

"Biblical symbolism. The Major said. "The Heathen is trying to tell me that no amount of mammon will..."

A high-pitched screaming sliced through the Major's explanation. They all looked to see Dogbite hopping about and flailing one arm like a little girl having a fit. The coins all but forgotten.

The Major was riled up over being interrupted, but not as much as the little black rattlesnake that had latched onto Dogbite's hand.

"Stop your whining," Major Hertzig demanded.

But Dogbite's panic only grew until the Major killed him with a single well-aimed headshot. Dogbite fell backwards slowly and all at once. Like an ancient sequoia whose roots would no longer support its weight. A few of the hired men ignored him as they took pleasure in stomping the snake into tomorrow's soup.

"Father?"

"Yes?"

"It looks like he almost killed you," Wesley said, *"symbolically,* that is."

CHAPTER XXI

THE SIEGE

D ays went by before darkness came.

Wesley was in a unique position to watch it all unfold. Lamed-up and the Major's only living son made it so no one asked him for anything. He looked on as their spirit broke, in degrees, one at a time and each to a different extent.

They had made a horrible mistake. Most were just bullies and thugs, while the best of them were bushwhackers. Men who would dictate their battles as quick, brutal things and near always on horseback. They struck like lightning and were gone before the fires were put out. But this was a siege. Something akin to getting hawks to swim after a sea monster. And no one saw it but him.

They kept up firing, mostly at shadows or what they thought-they-saws.

One man, driven mad by the loss of his only friend, shot every cartridge he had and started throwing anything not bolted down out at the Four Bits and the hated man hiding within.

It took five men to pull him down. They, his own comrades, started punching and kicking him until the Major tossed them away in their ones and twos.

Another had bled out. He stayed at his post and continued firing as his life quietly ebbed away.

The calm between exchanges was even harder to some. It gave them time to contemplate their worth as they waited to see who would be the next to die.

The supplies had returned with only a few cartridge boxes and not much else but excuses. The town had been hulled out. Some towners had told how Jack had bought most everything that was worth a damn and hauled it into the Four Bits.

Doc Geraint had gotten lost or hid out in a bottle before he could be useful, so Wesley stood in for the bullet-patching. His only experience was what he had witnessed in makeshift field hospitals. He was better than a cork and a mallet, but not by much. The second amputation became a nightmare. The screaming started when the carpenter's tools were laid out. And Wesley couldn't stop the spraying gore.

"Stop firing," Wesley yelled out, over and over until they had ceased. "Father?"

The Major looked worn to a nub and a terror all at once. He hadn't slept the night before, waiting for his house to be attacked, or snuck into. He still hadn't found Justine and that had to be twisting up his guts into a noose. Wesley handed his father a Winchester. At first glance, it looked as if their enemy had pulled off an amazing shot, one that had punched through the firing chamber.

"Father."

But the Major already understood. It had cost him one man, but it took another man's face before they figured it out. It was the ammo that Longhorn had found. 'Just the few boxes.' In the caliber they needed. And it was spiked. The heathen had probably replaced the black powder with dynamite- the same dynamite that he'd used the night before on his bunkhouse.

Wesley could do nothing to help. The man stood dumbfounded. His hand cupped the tattered side of his face and eyesocket.

"Where'd we get the shells?" Major Hertzig asked Longhorn.

"Cartman's."

"Remind me to kill that dirty little Jew when this is all said and done."

"Won't it be easier if I just remind you of the few you'll let live?" his son answered.

The sneak attack returned. One leaning on the other. Blood leaked from between his fingers as he tried to cover his eyeball. They reported to the Major.

"Well?"

"I got snakebit."

The Major looked him over. "What happened to your eye?"

"I got snakebit."

"Honest, Major," the unhurt one said, "they was nailed up by their tails, hangin' upside down like drying laundry, in the winder. When Ike parted the curtains, he got chomped."

"Where the hell is he getting all these snakes?"

"From you," Longhorn informed the Major, "I mean, they're yours. Dogbite bagged up some of your fighting snakes for Sal. To make the Injun pay for shaming us."

"Where's Sal?" Major Hertzig asked. "If anyone can sneak up and kill this bastard, it'll be Sal."

"Sal's dead," Longhorn told him, "Looks like he was snuck up on and killed."

Wesley looked at the two injured men, standing next to each other, both with a hand covering an eye and a more absurd irony he couldn't remember seeing. He chuckled to himself.

"You think this funny, boy?"

Wesley looked down at his gore covered suit and quietly said, "No, Father."

"Wes. Longhorn. Take two others and get the gun."

"The gun?"

"Yes. The cannon, Goddamn you, every shot, every shell and every grain of powder!"

"Father, if you do this, the townsfolk will never forgive you."

When I am done here," Major Hertzig said, sounding done in, "they will beg for my forgiveness."

"But Father..."

The Major cut him off with a gesture. "If he wants a war, I'll give him one that Achilles himself would shy away from."

Chapter XXII

Saviors, Skip Shot & Shell

It was well after midnight when the column of Federals arrived at the outskirts of Calvary.

"The town appears normal," Lieutenant Kilpatrick said as put his spyglass away. He wore his disappointment poorly, as if he wanted to arrive just as the town was being put to the torch.

Pitt remained silent. Too tired to argue.

The Lieutenant started buffing his uniform's brass and buttons. "Well, we've ridden this far. We shouldn't keep the ladies waiting any longer."

"We should send in a scout," Corporal Osburn said, still trying to see anything out of the ordinary.

"I already *scouted* with my field glass."

"You ever seen combat, Sir?"

The Lieutenant whirled. He was not accustomed to having guff from the ranks. Back during the War none of the enlisted in his supply depot would have ever talked to him in such a fashion.

"Yes, Corporal, I have."

"Was it through that fancy spyglass?"

Kilpatrick waved the column forward and said in a low tone, "Sergeant Graves used to question my orders too...."

They entered from the South and went straight up the main street. A few watched from the safety of their storefronts. A bag of feminine wrinkles smoking a clay pipe made the sign of the cross as they passed, but said nothing.

"They're in the church," came a yell from a well-hidden man. To most Texans, having bluebellies ride in to save them was like finding out their grandmother was a really good kisser.

The Lieutenant trotted forward, turning his horse just so at the large glass storefronts where he imagined young ladies would get a good look. He stopped, touched up his dash with the help of his own reflection and waved his command onward.

They came to a halt in front of the church, where a full bore Confederate artillery Major sat on the steps. Red kerchief and all.

Kilpatrick stopped the column and threw a quick salute. This was the closest he'd ever been to an enemy. He could see the headlines all the way back in Boston, "Last Confederate Surrenders his Sword." This was the stuff of promotions. Or even the beginning of a political career.

"Smells like a battlefield, Lieutenant."

"Shut up, Osburn, I'm in charge here."

The Major stood up and saluted with an unhurried smoothness.

Lieutenant sent back another one, with starch. "I am here to accept your surrender, Sir."

The Major chuckled. Haggard and wound tighter than a thirty dollar pocket watch. "Ok. What are your terms?"

The Lieutenant wasn't sure what had happened here, or why. All that could be fussed through once he had secured his prisoners. And his future.

"Lay down your arms and come out in an orderly fashion."

Someone from inside cracked open one of the church's doors.

"Can I have your terms in writing?"

"But of course, Sir," The Federal officer started fishing around in his saddlebags for paper and ink.

"Are we going to find cover, or just sit here?"

"I swear Osburn, one more outburst from you and I'll have your stripes. Can't you see that this is a matter for gentlemen?"

The Major slipped back into the church as the Federal officer pulled out his writing gear.

Kilpatrick hunched over, blocking off the rain the best he could as he rapidly scribbled away. Worried that his men, or possibly the Major's, might louse it up.

"There, I'm done," the Lieutenant said triumphantly as the church doors swung open and he could not understand why he was looking down the barrel of a cannon. And he died.

The Napoleon fired. It's makeshift doubleload of nails, debris and pieces of stained glass devastated the entire column. Those who weren't killed outright were maimed, or were shot before they could recover their wits. Point blank and in the open, they were slaughtered.

The Major's men hooted and hollered. Part payback for the war and part because now they wouldn't be shot up from two sides at once. Morale soared as they rushed out to loot, stepping about the pieces of horse and man.

Major Hertzig and his son watched from the safety of the church's entrance.

"You don't seem worried about him sneaking up on us?" Wesley asked.

"No. He knows how easy it'd be to kill him once he's away from that turtle shell he's hiding in," the Major answered. "But I ain't going to sleep, not with dawn just a few hours off."

"Now we start shelling?"

"Not yet. It's still too dark to hit anything."

Gunfire broke out and the Major's crew was culled a few more. Small fires, started by the cannon shot, had lit up the looters.

The Major ordered covering fire from his men still manning the rifle ports.

Those who weren't hit, crawled through the mud back to the church. Some lost their rifles, but there were plenty inside that were blood spattered and gathering dust.

The Major went further back into the church as Wesley watched them struggle their way out of the line of fire.

"Is it still too dark?"

With the predawn light, the Major released the hellfire. Flame and smoke accompanied the thunderous blast as twelve pounds of lead shattered one of the whorehouse's chimneys.

"No, dammit, skip shot it," the Major told the crew.

"What the hell's that?" Longhorn said. He had been taught a lot by Buck, but "skip shot" wasn't part of it.

"Aim low, about three quarters of the way to the target. It'll skip like a rock on a pond."

"I never threw a twelve pound hunk of lead into a puddle."

Longhorn did it. And it was devastating.

The next shot skipped, sending up a brilliant fantail of water and mud each time it bounced. It smashed into the Four Bits, tearing away a ragged hole as it continued inside.

They had busted out a beautiful stained glass of the Resurrection for a gunport and slid a door over the opening between shots, to save the crew from counter rifle-fire. Shot after hot. With a sound like trees snapping, a chunk of the second floor collapsed, bringing forth cheers and hats waving, until another of the Major's riflemen fell dead from the sharpshooter's talent.

A dozen cannon shots later, the Major ordered a pause. He had Longhorn watch as he filled the gold-plated shell casing with lead ball and powder. He went on to punch a hole in the Borman fuse and pack the shell. The class ended there as the Pastor stood at the entranceway.

"That is enough," Hiram commanded, pointing a finger at the Major, "Get out of God's house."

"You're not needed or wanted. Go away," the Major said.

"It's over. Right here, right now."

"You go straight to Hell."

"I'll be back. And I'll bring with me every man who can pull a trigger or hold a torch. We'll burn you out and shoot any who try and run." There was no bluff to the Pastor's words.

"Wait. I want this over as badly as you," the Major put on his honeyed voice, "You want to end this? Then please, you go out and reason with him."

"I'll go with you, Pastor," Wesley volunteered.

"What?" his father asked.

"You said it yourself. He won't shoot while we have a white flag."

"Now why would you want to do that?"

"I need to."

"You ask him if he knows where Justine is. You try and get my deeds back. Those slips of paper are ownership to more land than some European countries. And you make damn sure to get back our family heritage."

Wesley rolled up his gunbelt, left it on his makeshift operating table and picked up the white flag from where Dogbite had flung it.

"When this is over, I'll take you to Mexico. I'll buy ten ladies to take care of your every need."

"First, one must last," Wesley said as he kept walking.

"Damn, son, you're starting to sound like him," the Major said, pointing his thumb towards the whorehouse.

"You don't understand at all, Father. I'm already dead."

They picked their way through the mud and bodies.

Hiram supporting the stiff-limping Wesley as they made their way.

"Oh, and Pastor," the Major yelled, "you can ask him to lie down and die."

Once they were out of earshot, the Major grabbed one of his men. "Take a couple of torches and toss one into each back window. He can't be chattin' away with my son and putting out fires at the same time."

xXx

The Pastor held up. About the same spot where Dogbite had, but there was no reaction from within. From some of the gaps and holes leaked grain. Or sand. Making the whorehouse look like it was bleeding from her mortal wounds.

"Hello?"

They waited.

"Can we approach?"

"What do you want?"

"I'd like to give you a letter, for Sara. I need to apologize to her. I'm sorry that she and her son got hurt." Wesley slowly pulled it out of his coat pocket. "Can the Pastor give it to you?"

"Come on inside."

They hadn't expected that and hesitated. "Aren't you afraid I'll shoot you or something?"

"I do not think either of us are afraid."

Wesley entered, followed closely by the Pastor.

"Never thought I'd be caught dead in this place," Hiram said. "Sorry. Didn't mean anything by it."

Morgan looked chewed up and only half spat out. Sitting just a few yards away, covered in a thick layer of grain and sand. He was bandaging his thigh. A doctor's field kit lay open next to him. The bullet wound was only stitches and pain now.

The bloody bullet sat on a small table alongside a pile of cut-off rattlesnake rattles. Wesley shook his head, one mystery cleared up.

"Have a seat."

Wesley was amazed at the man's calm. And it brought up memories of the church steps when they had met. More astounding was how the Four Bits' interior looked.

The place had had all the frivolous trappings removed. Bags of sand and grain lined the entire front wall with lumber reenforcing. Rifle-ports were fashioned throughout, at odd heights. When not in use, a red painted bag covered each hole, to keep out any uninvited bullets. But it was made to hold out rifle fire, not cannonballs. Whole areas had collapsed, and the insides were busted up pretty good.

"I haven't seen too many of those," Wesley pointed to the Whitworth sitting close by. "Did you take that off a dead man during the War?"

"No, I killed a couple for it," Morgan answered. "Have I hurt any of the civilians?"

"No. Dogbite lied to you," Wesley said, "there are no townsfolk in the church."

Morgan pulled out a yellow handled razor and sliced a few sandbags.

"So, what now?"

"You go back," Morgan said, "and more die."

166

The Pastor billed in. "You're not thinking straight. You probably haven't slept a wink in at least two days."

Morgan started to put together the makings for a small fire on the bed of sand he'd made.

"You can't possibly stand up to these odds. They will kill you sure as the sun will rise."

"I came here to kill a man." Morgan pulled out a block of matches, but they were crushed. And wet. He had killed them too. "Or die."

Wesley handed him his.

"Thanks," Morgan said, striking the match on the first try. He picked up a bloody medical tool and pinched one of his Sharpshooting bullets.

"You could ride away. My father doesn't have enough men left to come after you."

"Where would I get a horse?"

xXx

Major Hertzig watched as Hiram plodded through the rain and mud back towards the Church. "What's going on? Where's my son?"

"He's still in there. Where's your horse?"

"Why?"

"Wesley worked out a trade."

"For what?" The Major had his suspicions.

"The stolen papers."

"And what does the 'breed get in return?"

"A horse."

"A horse?"

"Not just any horse, he wants *your* big gray."

"My..." The Major couldn't believe it. "For a horse?" He started to laugh. Unless his enemy had grown mighty hungry, a horse meant only one thing. The end was in sight.

xXx

Wesley and the Pastor walked back to the church in silence, each to his own thoughts. Hiram had delivered the horse and Wesley had a carpetbag chock full of papers.

From the Four Bits came a sound like a wounded turkey bleating. There was a rhythm to it, a warbling pain-filled thing that struck a cord of remorse.

The Major walked partway out to meet them. A piece of white sheet tied to the end of his rifle. He looked elated at what they'd done, happier than anytime since this all had started.

"It's over. That's a bonafided Cherokee death rattle. He's telling his ancestors that he's coming."

"Go back to the church, Father, before you get shot." He handed over the bag.

The Major looked at his son as if he was daft. "He's cost me everything. I have to be the one to kill him."

"Why? You got your kingdom back?"

The Major held up a fistful of a blind man's sheet music, the contents from the carpetbag.

"You are so damned naive."

"I'm sorry about last night. I do love you," the son told his father.

"I know, boy." Johannes bit back saying more, "Did he say where Justine is?"

"I didn't ask."

The Major let it go, for the moment, as he grabbed Hiram. "I need your services."

"Father!"

"Shut up boy. When that song stops, he'll come out to meet his ancestors." The Major's good mood returned. "And I'll be here to see that he does."

CHAPTER XXIII

RETRIBUTION

Johannes Hertzig was wet. And cold. And wrung out. Everything that mattered to him had been destroyed or had come up missing. Only through the death of this heathen, at his very own hands, could he start to make things right again in his world. So he advanced. Into the no man's land between the church and the whorehouse. He hid behind Hiram. Using the man of the cloth as a two-legged shield.

The Major watched as smoke billowed from the Four Bits. The unmistakable crackle of a large fire could clearly be heard as it ate deep from the brothel's insides.

Hertzig had not made fifty yards from the church when three shots and a high-pitched rebel holler came from deep within the Four Bits as the Major's big gray burst out of the batwing doors. The gray clad rider, blackened by powder and covered in a thick layer of dirt, black hair flowing from underneath the battered hat, hunkered low in the saddle. A neckerchief about the nose helped against the smoke that billowed forth from the depths of the interior. But it was the vicious heavyset Lemats held tight in each gauntleted fist that garnered the Major's attention.

The Pastor was tossed away, no longer needed as the Major readied his rifle, the white linen still tied to the barrel.

The Major held his fire, taking careful aim and allowing the distance to close. The Winchester '66 levered with ease as the Major blazed through the entire tube of .44 caliber rimfires.

The Major's lead cut the charge short. Mount and rider tumbled, rolled and crunched into a grisly tangled heap.

But the Major didn't stop. Too many years of Indian fighting had taught him to make damn sure his enemy wasn't playing possum. He jerked the massive Walker from the over-sized flap holster. The horse pistol spoke quickly. The first round smashed into the horse's underside. As the bay's head rose up in pain a second round silenced the horse forever. The animal's weight pinned the rider. Hertzig fired again, hitting the motionless rider's exposed leg. The Major started to laugh. He had won. But Johannes continued, skirted clockwise and came around from the rear. When he had a clear shot he took it, and another, into the rider's back. The bullets struck true, but with no visible effect.

The rider was dead.

Major Hertzig advanced a step, took pleasure in his aim, and placed his last shot into the back of the skull.

xXx

Wesley eased the binoculars down and rubbed his eyes. "Stand down," he ordered, both relieved and somewhat disappointed, "it's over."

The cannoneers stopped with the gun half-loaded. They slid open the shield-door to see what they'd done. And to let out some of the infernal smoke. Some cheered, others sat down or laid out. To rest. Or to think about what they had just lived through.

xXx

The Major was puzzled. Advanced. The closer he drew the more bewildered he became. It was all wrong. A sickly, disgusting void opened up inside him. Swallowed him and spat him to his knees. The constant rain started to remove the black paint from her long red hair. It was the same paint that their bullets had chipped off from the false widow openings. Part of her forehead had left with her father's last

170

shot, reminding him of his own wound that had never healed. Even in death, she still wore her hatred. The fall had yanked the kerchief down to reveal the taut gag. The pistols, like her body, were tied in place.

xXx

Wes saw his father crumple to his knees but didn't understand why. He raised the field glasses up when he caught the faintest of sounds. A wooden heartbeat sounded twice over the subtle melody of the rain. The batwing doors had swung open and hinged back to rest.

From deep inside the darkness he came. Through the black smoke that poured from the mouth of the parlor house. Shirtless, shoeless, and armed with his sabre and English rifle. He slammed the sword's point down into the walkway, took a knee behind it. Morgan threaded the Whitworth's barrel through the sabre's "D" shaped handguard, supporting the rifle's aim.

"Load! God damn it, Load!" Wesley screamed as he pointed at the Four Bits. The desperate order galvanized the crew into action. Buck had trained them well. To a man, they worked as one.

The riflemen in the church cut loose a ragged volley at first. Swiftly the rapid-fire of the lever actions increased into a maelstrom.

xXx

Morgan prepared with the precision forged upon countless battlefields. Angry lead buzzed about, wood splinters from the hitching rail, support posts and overhang, twisted and turned into shrapnel that left nasty little gashes in their wake. Or jabbed at him like an army of miniature spear-toting Persians against a Titan.

The Major's grief-stricken features were clearly seen through the Davidson scope. So close. Morgan felt the trigger's cool metal as he took up its slack. He paused and his eyes squeezed shut, for something soft had brushed against the back of his other hand.

Something silky.

Something blue.

Morgan realigned the Whitworth's aim point. It was a difficult shot.

More than four hundred yards. The predawn light varied from the rain swept street into the shadowed interior of the church. Without enough light the long brass scope became useless, forcing him to use the iron sights.

In their revelry at killing the Indian, they'd let down their guard. Morgan had a chance. A slim one, but a chance.

The rain itself a factor. And the pain.

Morgan's target was partially protected by the wood and bronze of the twelve pounder's carriage and barrel. If the shot ran true, it would strike the pinewood ammunition chest that sat atop the limber.

The preheated bullet would punch through to ignite dozens of powder bags. It was the same bullet that Wesley had watched him make a fire for.

All movement stopped. Not even a breath. As if an ancient god had transformed him into a statue. Pressure crept from finger to trigger until the spring loaded hammer crashed down on the copper primer cap, causing a small amount of fulminate of mercury instantly to release a burst of hot gas into the main charge, sending the .451 caliber elongated "hot shot" down the hexagonal barrel. The bullet screamed along a razor straight path.

xXx

Longhorn's aversion to labor had been replaced with a quickness born out of bigotry, humiliation and vengeance. He leapt in front of the cannon's muzzle to load the hollow cased gold-plated shell. The newfound work ethic cost him his life as the well aimed bullet tore through his upper torso from behind. The force sent him colliding face first into the gun tube, shattering the cowhand's lopsided buck teeth. He dropped, already a corpse.

Wesley scooped up and loaded the bloody cannon shell. It was only a matter of time until this mess would be over. The whorehouse would soon be a funeral pyre. Leg shot and without a horse ruled out escape. And he could not hold his ground. His fate was sealed.

Morgan stood up and tossed the rifle into the flooded street. Drew his sabre from the boardwalk and advanced like the Greeks at Marathon.

"My God," Wes said.

"What's he doing?"

"He's attacking."

The Major's riflemen kept up the fusillade, determined to take down this one man.

A bullet creased along the top of Morgan's ear, carrying away a strand of hair with it.

But he continued.

Lightning sliced down from the heavens. Thunder bellowed. The downpour intensified.

But he continued.

A second bullet struck Morgan. Solid. He dropped without ceremony, disappearing beneath the small rainwater lake.

The gunfire slowed until it came to a complete stop. The only sounds that could be heard above the rain was the Major cursing God for making him kill his own daughter.

Townsfolk who had watched from warm and safe places hesitantly ventured outside to see for themselves what this night had wrought. And some of them were armed now.

The first ray of daylight broke across the landscape, revealing the battered town's fresh scars. Most of the filth had yielded to the storm. From where Morgan had gone down in the dirty brown waters, that selfsame beam of light caught and flickered.

The sword.

Wesley's eyes burned with the glare. That damned sword. Flames from the Four Bits shone from the blade, twisting its reflection into a hellish sight.

Wes watched in disbelief as the Indian struggled to a knee and labored to fill his lungs. The muddy water coursed off him as he struggled to his feet. Unsteady, sword and man resumed their attack.

The rifles spoke of death again.

In another time, in another place, Wesley would have been proud to know such a man. Maybe comrades-in-arms or perhaps even friends. He doffed his hat and held it high.

"What élan!" Wesley cried as he yanked the firing lanyard.

The church disappeared in a double impact of explosions that rocked the entire town. Bits of brick and wood outraced the fireball that engulfed the building. Flames billowed upward until they lost themselves in a vicious oily cloud of smoke.

With Longhorn's death, Buck's teachings died. Wesley's infantry officer's skills were meaningless to the proper handling of a fieldpiece. The fuse plug on the explosive shell had been rammed directly against the powder bag.

Wesley's yank had set off the main powder charge, blasting the fuse into the gunpowder and iron shot held within the hollow of the shell. It ripped apart still within the Napoleon. Large chunks of bronze cannon, shell casing and shot burst outwards, setting off more than forty neatly-arranged powder bags inside the ammunition chest.

The smoke drifted and thinned to reveal the devastation left in the explosion's wake. Little still stood of the church. Hundreds of individual fires competed with the rain for the church's scattered remains.

Both men looked away from the spectacle and turned their attention to each other.

Morgan started for the Major. His stranglehold on the saber softened, and the supple blade lowered into a practiced low guard.

The Major's eyes saw only the past as the Indian slogged closer. Everything he was, his power, his respectability, and now his baby girl, were all gone. He tasted the putrid bile of remorse for the first time in his life. His sins took shape in the lifeless body he cradled. The sword slumbered in the Major's sheath.

Most of the town poured out into the rain to watch this come to an end. Isabella de Anza was there. Mr. Cartman too.

The rainfall eased up somewhat.

Morgan came to a stop just beyond the Major's reach and tossed the sword away. His hand speared forward, caught the Major's kerchief and plucked it off, revealing the mass of scar tissue and scabs. The scalping had never healed right. Blood started to well up. The pain brought the Major back to the here and now. He squirmed to look back at the half-breed.

"You've won. So now what?" The Major could barely make out Morgan's face, but it was enough.

Morgan's free hand went to the small of his back and brought forth Nemesis.

"You can't kill me in front of all these people. You'll be branded a murderer," he said in a reasonable fashion.

The pistol's icy touch against the back of his head was the only reply.

"Think what this will do to you."

In his mind's eye, Major Johannes Dietrich Hertzig saw what he would do. This was just a setback. With his money and lands he'd grab power by the horns once again. Burn Calvary down around their ungrateful ears. Maybe it was his calling to teach them a biblical lesson. He could rebuild the town in a spiritual fashion. Double the size of the church. Hire a small army, if need be, until he had the renegade half-breed's head on a silver platter. Then he'd be free to remarry... maybe even have another child. Perhaps a daughter!

"This was never about me."

Nemesis roared.

CHAPTER XXIV

THE HEALING

Morgan woke up not knowing....
All stiff and sore.

Covered in bandages and not in chains. He made sure of that before anything else.

And he was warm.

And Sara lay half draped over him. She was asleep and breathing softly. Her hair had pooled into a small nest on his shoulder.

Sunlight streamed in from an open window, so bright that Morgan fought to open his eyes. A cool breeze played with the curtains as it caressed Morgan's face.

There was a tapping and Jack came in. He was all new clothes and smiles.

"Damnit. Looks like you're going to live."

Morgan tried to smile.

"Well... you up for listening to some womanly gossip?" Jack said as he pulled up a stool. He pulled out his bag of fixings. "You've been napping away for the better part of three days now. Never have I seen such a lazy bunch of bones."

"Pitt died with the bluecoats, so the townsfolk made Mr. Cartman to be the "interim Mayor" until they can get a real election up and running."

Sara started to wake.

"The Pastor donated a wagonfull of money to help people rebuild and is out lending a hand to anyone who needs it.

His church meetings are now held under a tent, and his flock has more than doubled. Heck, I've even started going."

"What about Sara?"

"Doc says Sara's going to be fine. He don't know how much voice she'll get back, but she'll live, no doubt about that." Jack's smile got even dopier. "What about you?"

"When will I be arrested?"

"What for? You helped in the apprehension of a vile outlaw gang."

Infection had set in alongside a terrible fever. It had broken now, but had left Morgan weak and more than a little confused.

"It says so in the official report already sent to Austin."

"And the Major?"

"Haven't you heard? He's dead." Jack said, "Shot while trying to escape from the new Sheriff."

"I will not be a Sheriff."

Jack laughed. "Nope, you can't have my job." He pulled his jacket back enough to show off the tin star pinned to his vest.

"Oh yeah, the Circle Nine was put to the match." Jack lit up the thin cigar.

Morgan looked on as Jack flamed up his smoke.

"I suspect it was Ms. de Anza, so I'll be keeping a close eye on her from now on. Matter-a-fact, we're going on a buggy ride this evening."

Morgan tried to sit up, but was defeated. Too weak and too bandaged.

"I better go and check on my deputy. He's a good man, but he never smiles, leastways not that one could tell from under that huge moustache of his. You might remember him... he was on the stage? Anyways, I'll let Alex in now. He's guarded your door ever since we brought you in."

Jack got up and paused, looking at the best friend he ever had. The man he felt he owed his new grubstake on life. "Thanks." Jack left.

Alexander flew onto the bed, without waiting or warning, waking up his mother and hurting Morgan. And nothing could have felt better.

Morgan stiffened, awkward at the situation, but her eyes told me that he didn't need to be.

"I am not half the woman I was when we met," came the strained whisper of her voice.

"You sacrificed yourself to save your son. You are now twice the woman I first met."

"But my voice... it may never...."

Morgan gently placed his finger on her lips. "Then I will never raise my voice to you."

Sara cuddled deeper against him and Morgan was whole.

"You came back to us," Alex said, proud that he had been right about everything.

"That depends on your mother."

"We go where you go," she said without hesitation, "after all, we are a family."

"I have something I must do. It could be dangerous," Morgan told her in the sternest of tones. "You can not come."

After all, Morgan thought, a man must define what's what within his marriage.

xXx

Chief Stand Watie. Warrior. Statesman. And former Brigadier General of the Confederate States of America, rose from his front porch rocker to see for himself the covered wagon coming up his drive.

Yesterday he had been told that they were coming, so he went to the chair and waited.

Hundreds had gathered. They had started to arrive the afternoon before. Setting up shelters of hide and surplus tentage. People set out their wares and music drifted throughout. By evening, there was dancing and in the morning, there was a ball-game, with each contestant carrying the traditional playing stick, brightly painted with symbols to bestow special powers.

And still, Stand Watie remained at his post. The wagon was closer now, and the old Chief could clearly make out the three of them. He did not know the little boy or the lady, but there was no mistaking Morgan Black, grandson of Kills-in-Water, son of Arthur Black, and the boy who was a warrior before he was old enough to be a man. His short-cropped hair and civilian storeboughts could not hide his identity from Watie. What concerned the old mountain lion was those who still wore the crossed pins that mixed with the assembled crowd, but were not there for the festivities.

The crowd grew silent as they parted, like the Red Sea, before the slow moving wagon. It came to a halt, Morgan set the brake, jumped down and helped the woman and child down.

Watie came to them and hugged Morgan as if he were his own son.

They separated to arm's length and the old warrior looked from Morgan's dress shoes to his short cropped hair.

"Is the War of Northern Aggression finally over?" asked the last Southern General to surrender.

Morgan smiled his answer. "This is Sara, my wife," he scruffed the boy's hat. "And this is Alexander, our son."

Alex looked up with his mouth open, shyness taking his voice.

The boy held a carved wooden locomotive tight to his chest. Freshly painted a bright red and with six new brass wheels. Wheels that a fully grown man could present for a couple of days worth of pleasure at the Four Bits. Alex knew none of this. It was enough that his toy was shiny and that it rolled well. And that both his dads had made it just for him. It was his most prized possession.

"It is my pleasure to meet the lady who captured this man."

"Thank you," she said in a whisper.

Morgan turned and pulled his sheathed Prussian saber from underneath the wagon's seat. With both hands, he handed it to Watie.

"Why?"

"I do not need it anymore."

"So it is mine?"

"Yes."

The old warrior carefully took hold of the sharpened steel. "Has your son been given his Cherokee name?"

"Not yet."

"Then we shall do so." The Chieftain turned to the boy.

"After the naming ritual it is tradition for you to receive a gift. My gift to you will be this sword. It belonged to a great man once," Stand Watie said, "it was given to him by his grandfather."

The old man's happiness became awe as Morgan brought forth another sword from the same place. It was as ordinary looking as the mountains or a sunrise. A standard cavalryman's weapon. But the old Chieftain knew what it was. Who it had belonged to. And what it represented to his people.

Stand Watie reverently took hold of the saber and after staring at it for a long moment, feeling its cold weight in his hands, he held it up for all to see.

The hills of their new lands had never heard such a cheering.

Those who still wore the pins were embarrassed. This day would not be theirs. One look from the warrior-Chieftain-elder, and they mounted up and left, without a word. The last one turned and bowed his head before joining the others.

The old man smiled.

Sometimes, a sword can heal.

THE SWORD

Some would say none of this story is real. Or some would argue that Texans took honor from the field at the Battle of Neches, and not grisly trophies carved from the body of an 83 year-old Cherokee Chief.

But if one wants to see for oneself an unadorned sword. The sword that weathered the Civil War and the Battle of Neches. The sword given by General Sam Houston to Chief Bowles on February 23, 1836. The sword that was taken after a Militia Captain placed the barrel of his pistol against the back of the Chief's head and pulled the trigger, one would have to travel to the city of Tahlequah, in the former Indian Territories... and respectfully request permission from the members of the oldest Masonic lodge in Oklahoma-

-where it is displayed on a simple plywood shelf.